W9-ATL-115

The Hooker,
the Dancer
and the Nun

Other books by John D. Mills:

Reasonable and Necessary
The Manatee Murders
The Objector
Sworn Jury
The Trophy Wife Divorce

The Hooker,
the Dancer
and the Nun

by

John D. Mills

Pono

www.PonoPubs.com

This book is a work of fiction. Names, character, places, and incidents either are the product of the author's imagination or are used fictitiously, and any resemblance to actual persons, living or dead, business establishments, events, or locales is entirely coincidental.

Copyright ©2015 John D. Mills
All rights reserved. No part of this book may be reproduced, stored in a retrieval system, or transmitted by any means, electronic, mechanical, photocopying, recording, or otherwise without written permission from the author.

Library of Congress Control Number: TBA

ISBN -13: 978-1519339195
ISBN -10: 1519339194

Printed in the United States
Second Edition

Editor: Megan Parker, Calliope & Quill
Layout and editing: Inge Heyer

Cover art and map of Pine Island Sound: Cameron Graphics

Pono Publishing
Laramie, Wyoming
Hilo, Hawai`i

www.PonoPubs.com

Acknowledgements

I would like to thank my lovely wife, Paula Lynn Mills, for her support and patience while writing this novel. I couldn't have completed it without her constant encouragement and helpful editing. My life, and my love of writing, have both improved substantially since she came into my life.

I would also like to thank the following people who helped me edit, design, format, and publish this book:

Angela Savko
Jackie Mills
Bill Mills
Joy Mills
Anna McDaniel
Megan Parker
Sheryl Riebenack
Connie Serrano
John Hendricks
Beth Maliszewski
Stephanie J. Slater
Timothy F. Slater
Inge Heyer

Pine Island

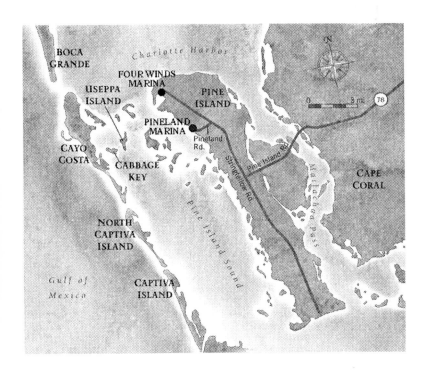

Pine Island is the largest island off Florida's Gulf Coast,
located in Lee County in southwest Florida.

Prologue

August 15, 1995 at 4:14 p.m.

Gator Zone Apartments in Gainesville, Florida

"The Nun has another date with the cute Sigma Nu over in building 12. Do you think she'll give it up tonight?" Susan Kelly asked playfully.

Lacy Turner laughed. "She tells us she's saving herself for marriage, but he's really cute. I guess it depends on how much tequila he gets in her."

Susan and Lacy had just finished unloading the U-Haul truck they had used to move all of their belongings from the freshman dorms to an off-campus three bedroom apartment they were sharing with the Nun. Susan nodded as she opened up a U-Haul box sitting on the kitchen counter and began unloading dishes. "I can't believe she made it through our freshman year untouched with all the hunks that were chasing her. I think the University should give her a special award."

Lacy scooped out silverware from her opened box and remarked, "I'm proud of her. She said she was going to wait until Mr. Right came along, and so far she's done it."

The air conditioner was struggling in the summer heat and Susan was getting hot and sticky. She pulled her long curly red hair back into a ponytail and grabbed a rubber band from the kitchen counter to hold it in place. "Oh, well. That just means more men for me."

Lacy shook her head and said cheerfully, "Listen here, Dancer, I think you've had more than your fair share of the studs on campus. Every time you go out on the dance floor and shake that prize booty of yours, a new guy becomes infatuated with you."

Susan laughed and said coyly, "I was always told that blondes have more fun, but you've been blowing off all the guys that have been hitting on you lately. You're gonna get cobwebs down there if you don't use it."

Lacy sighed. "I need to change perfume because the one I'm using apparently attracts all the losers. Why is it so difficult to find a good-looking guy with a nice boat to take me fishing on the weekends and take me to dinner during the week? Is that too much for a girl to ask for?"

Susan shook her head, smiling, and her red ponytail swished back and forth. They both finished unloading their boxes silently as they listened to Alanis Morissette sing "All I Really Want" on Susan's two foot long boom box on the coffee table.

The front door opened. Patricia Hendricks walked in

2

with two grocery bags loaded with frozen pizzas, chips and ice cream, and she said cheerfully, "It feels so good to walk into an apartment that I share with my best friends!"

"The Nun returns to our den of sin," Lacy said amusingly.

Patricia set the bags down on the kitchen table and pointed at Lacy as she smiled. "When is the Hooker going to get a new boyfriend so she can enjoy our den of sin?"

"Sometimes, I'd just rather go fishing than listen to all of the lines from the frat boys at the bars. I need a real man to come along and make my toes curl." Lacy said optimistically.

Lacy Turner was from Everglades City and grew up fishing the backwaters with her father on their flats boats. She was a tall girl with sun bleached sandy blonde hair from her years of fishing and being on the high school swim team. Her green eyes were made even brighter by her dark tan. She was studying psychology and working as a waitress at the local Hooters to help pay her way through college. At work, she always lamented that she missed hooking big fish back home, so one of the other Hooters waitresses gave her the unflattering nickname, and it stuck.

Susan Kelly was from Miami and had grown up in a gated community in Coconut Grove. She was the only child of a successful stockbroker who spoiled her growing up, and continued to do so when Susan went to college. When she left Miami for her freshman year, her dad gave her a new red convertible 318i BMW and plenty of cash to shop and party. She was a petite, curvy redhead that kept herself in shape with aerobics and jogging. She was majoring in physical education because all she really cared about was her looks and finding a husband to support her, just like her daddy.

Patricia Hendricks was from Tampa and had attended Catholic schools. She was a pretty girl with an average build, fair skin, raven hair and brown eyes. Her parents made certain she lived a sheltered life and didn't allow her to date in high school. However, she thrived under the structured lifestyle because she enjoyed school and learning. When her fifteenth birthday was approaching, she had asked for a file cabinet for her birthday gift. She decided in her senior year of high school that she wanted to teach special education in an elementary school, so she went to the University of Florida in Gainesville and enjoyed the excitement of a big school. However, she felt intimidated by the size of her classes.

Patricia picked up the grocery bags from the dining room table and walked into the kitchen to unload the food. "You won't believe who I ran into at Publix while I was grocery shopping . . . and what she told me!"

Susan looked at her expectantly and held her hands out to her side. "Don't keep us in suspense. Give us the dirt."

After a few seconds of enduring Patricia's mischievous

4

yet silent smile, Lacy held up her hands and shook them in mock rage. "Do we have to beg for it?"

"It's some good stuff," Patricia laughed. "You remember that crazy girl from chemistry class last year with the curly brown hair?"

Both Susan and Lacy nodded.

Patricia pulled out an eight inch by eleven inch piece of paper from the grocery bag and waived it dramatically. "Well, I saw her at Publix and she handed me a black and white copy of a nude Polaroid of the well-endowed president of Kappa Alpha!"

Susan lunged at the paper and took it from Patricia's hand for examination while Lacy looked over her shoulder in feverish curiosity. After a few seconds of close study, Susan nodded slowly. "It's authentic. I did him last semester when his girlfriend went away for the weekend."

Lacy snatched the picture from Susan and turned it upside down, looking closely at the details. "It looks like a cross between a zucchini and an Italian sausage."

Susan nodded knowingly and gave Lacy a naughty smile. "*He'll* make your toes curl."

Patricia giggled and Lacy was intrigued as she continued studying the picture closely.

"Where did this copy come from?" Susan asked.

Patricia said in a conspiratorial voice, "She said her roommate took the Polaroid while he was passed out in her

5

bed last night, and then this morning she went to Kinko's and make 100 copies and was passing them out on campus. She grabbed some from her and passed them out at Publix."

Susan was quiet for a few seconds while she thought about Polaroid shots of herself in old boyfriends' drawers and wondered if she should be concerned. Lacy quickly went to her bedroom and returned, playfully waiving a magnifying glass. Patricia and Susan giggled with delight at her determination. Lacy turned on all the lights in the dining room before she continued her examination of the photo.

Patricia pulled a large bottle of Patron Tequila from the kitchen cabinet and poured shots. "I think we all need to drink a shot to celebrate the start of our sophomore year!"

Chapter 1

Monday, August 17, 2015 at 9:04 a.m.

Courtroom 6B, Lee County Courthouse in Ft. Myers, Florida

"Ladies and gentlemen of the jury, during this murder trial you'll learn what drove the Defendant, Lacy Turner, to kill her college roommate, Susan Kelly, on a houseboat in Pine Island Sound. You'll also learn that on the night of the murder on the houseboat, a third college roommate, Patricia Hendricks, was present on the houseboat and went missing that night."

The prosecutor, Frank Powers, hesitated before he continued his opening statement, trying to entice the jury to want more details of the murder. He looked all of the jurors in the eyes as he gripped the podium.

"These three women were all former roommates at the University of Florida and lived in the same apartment for their sophomore, junior and senior years. Their nicknames in college were the Hooker, the Dancer and the Nun. The Defendant's nickname was the Hooker because she enjoyed fishing and hooking big fish. The victim's nickname was

7

the Dancer because she liked to go dancing at clubs. And the missing woman, her nickname was the Nun because she remained a virgin during her college years."

Frank noticed two of the female jurors on the front row glanced at each other with disapproving nods, but two of the male jurors seated behind them in the second row glanced at each other with arched eyebrows and exchanged slight grins. Frank expected some strong feelings about the nicknames, so he wanted to bring them out first before the cutthroat defense attorney, Amanda Blayne, could try to use the nicknames to manipulate the jurors' feelings in her favor.

Frank continued in a somber tone. "For the past 20 years, these three women have remained connected. The missing friend, Patricia Hendricks, stayed close to the others all during this time and was referred to as 'the peacemaker' between the Defendant and the victim."

Frank was fifty-four and had been a prosecutor since he graduated from law school at age 25. He was five feet, eleven inches tall with graying hair and a trim build from riding his bicycle five miles daily. In his tenure at the State Attorney's Office, he had tried over 400 jury trials with a ninety two percent conviction rate, so he knew how to successfully create drama in the courtroom.

Frank stepped forward slightly and tightened his grip on the podium. He took a deep breath before he continued in a louder voice. "Sometimes, the Defendant and the victim

8

were the best of friends, but other times, they were bitter enemies because of a tangled romantic history. They had a problematic habit of dating some of the same men over the years. In addition, the Defendant briefly dated the victim's father and taunted her in texts and Facebook posts over her revenge love affair. As you can imagine, this created hostility between the two women. This hostility is ultimately what caused the Defendant to cut her former friend's throat and watch her horribly bleed to death on a houseboat."

Frank turned and pointed at Lacy Turner. "This woman lured the victim and their other friend, Patricia Hendricks, also known as the Nun, onto a houseboat for a supposed girls' weekend. All three college roommates had gotten divorced in the past year, and Lacy suggested they should reconnect during a weekend on the houseboat. In reality, it was her plan all along to isolate the victim and kill her."

"Objection!" Amanda Blayne announced loudly as she stood up. "The prosecutor is making arguments that he can't prove and he knows it! I request that he be held in contempt of court."

"Both counsel approach the bench." Judge Alexandra Bronson demanded firmly. She had been a judge for 20 years and knew how to handle trial attorneys that were pushing the rules of procedure. As the attorneys approached the bench, she shifted her glance toward the jurors and lowered her voice to a polite tone. "Ladies and gentlemen, during the trial I'll sometimes call a sidebar conference to consult with attorneys privately, and the rules of court require that you don't hear these conversations. During this time, I'll touch a button behind my bench here and the speakers in the ceiling above will play what is called 'white noise' to hopefully keep you from hearing our conversations."

Judge Bronson touched the button and smiled at the jurors before she turned and scowled at the attorneys waiting on the other side of her bench. Judge Bronson was a full figured, sixty year-old African-American who stood five feet, two inches tall. She'd begun her career as a public defender and had tried over a hundred cases before she was recruited by a law firm representing insurance companies because of her success in the courtroom. She'd tried over sixty jury trials defending against personal injury claims before she was appointed to the bench. She was well versed on how trial attorneys try to capture a jury's attention during opening statements and had developed her own method to keep attorneys from improperly grandstanding in her courtroom.

"Ms. Blayne," Judge Bronson said tersely, "I'm aware that you practice primarily in Miami and haven't tried any cases here in Lee County, so I'm putting you on notice that I don't allow speaking objections in my courtroom. Here, you state your objections and your grounds, and don't give any unneeded commentary. Do you understand?"

Amanda Blayne, a forty year-old attorney, had been

friends with Lacy during college. She was a five foot, nine inch bottle blonde with a pixie haircut and ran marathons year round. She had Nordic blue eyes, but used contacts with a yellow tint that transformed her eyes to a stunning turquoise blue. She'd been a state court prosecutor for five years and then became a federal prosecutor for seven years in Miami. She'd made the mistake of dating her married supervisor at the U.S. Attorney's Office, and when his wife found out, she created a very public spectacle and embarrassed Amanda. After a month of stress and co-workers looking over their shoulder at her, she decided to leave the U.S. Attorney's Office and hang her own shingle as a criminal defense lawyer. Over the past three years as a defense lawyer, she'd not lost a trial in Miami and she was determined to get her college friend acquitted at trial and gain good publicity for herself.

Amanda said matter-of-factly, "Your Honor, I don't think I made a speaking objection. I objected and then made a motion for contempt of court."

Judge Bronson took a deep breath and glared at Amanda while she thought of how to handle this challenge to her authority. Frank felt his neck pounding with heated blood and forced himself to concentrate and not get sidetracked from his planned opening statement. Everything he had heard about Amanda from his Miami prosecutor friends was true.

Judge Bronson crossed her arms on the bench and leaned

towards Amanda . "This is your first and only warning, Ms. Blayne. The next time you do a speaking objection, I'll fine you $500 for contempt of court. If you do it after that, I'll put you in jail for 10 days. Do I make myself clear?"

It wasn't the first time that Amanda had been threatened with jail and she secretly enjoyed pushing judges to their limits. However, she knew she had to say the right words on the record to help protect her zealous advocacy. "Your Honor, I'll follow your Order. Therefore, since we are now at side bar, I make a motion for contempt of court against the prosecutor."

"Your motion is denied! Your objection is denied!" Judge Bronson said sternly and pointed toward Amanda's side of the court. "Now go back to your table and let the prosecutor continue his opening statement without baseless objections from you."

Amanda was secretly happy that she had disrupted Frank's opening statement and that she'd let Judge Bronson know she wasn't backing down. Frank forced himself to concentrate on his opening statement and the evidence because he believed very strongly in his case. Both attorneys walked back to their prior position in the courtroom as Lacy looked hopefully at the jury. All of the jurors avoided eye contact with Lacy and looked instead at Judge Bronson.

Judge Bronson turned off the white noise and nodded towards Frank. "Mr. Powers, you may continue your opening statement."

Frank looked at the jurors as he gripped the podium and continued in a forceful tone. "The Defendant was in a drunken rage and sliced her friend's neck and then watched her die. After she committed the murder, she continued drinking until she blacked out. The Defendant was found passed out on a couch 12 feet from the bloody murder scene on the back deck of the houseboat. Her fingerprints were found on the bloody knife next to the victim by the sheriff's deputy that responded to a 911 call when the body was found floating in the water. The victim's blood splatter was all over the Defendant and the other woman on the houseboat is missing. These are uncontroverted facts that the two first responders saw at the gruesome murder scene aboard the houseboat."

Frank turned and stared at Lacy Turner as he continued in an accusatory voice. "We've subpoenaed Facebook posts and texts between these three ladies that had been deleted from the Defendant's computer and phone over the past year. Even though the communications were deleted, our computer experts were able to salvage one year of deleted Facebook posts and texts between these three ladies. Sadly, there are a number of disturbing posts and texts that establish multiple motives for murder and many threats made by the Defendant towards the victim."

Frank turned back toward the jury and lowered his

voice, "At the end of the trial, after you have heard all of the State's evidence, I'll ask you to find the Defendant guilty of second degree murder."

Frank walked back to his table and sat down as Judge Bronson looked at the defense table. "Does the Defense wish to present an opening statement?"

Amanda sprang to her feet and said emphatically, "We most certainly do, Your Honor." She walked decisively to the podium in her red pant suit and four-inch black leather high heels. "Ladies and gentlemen, Lacy didn't kill her friend, Susan. She'll testify and tell you everything she remembers about that night."

Amanda glanced at Lacy, nodded her head slowly, and gave her a reassuring smile. She looked back to the jury and pleaded with them, "My client and the victim had been drinking heavily that night and that's the last thing she remembers. Everyone was in a good mood because they'd taken Patricia's 19-foot boat over to a nearby island resort, Cabbage Key, for dinner and drinks. Remember, Patricia is the missing lady from the houseboat, and these ladies were like the modern day version of the Three Musketeers. It's true that they had their ups and downs over the years, but they'd been friends since they were freshmen in college."

Amanda took a deep breath and looked kindly at every juror before she continued. "There was a fishing tournament at Cabbage Key the next day, and there were over a hundred

14

fishermen on the island drinking and having a good time at the captain's meeting before the tournament began. All three of the ladies had met eligible men and planned on going back there the next night after a relaxing day at a nearby beach on Cayo Costa. Everyone was happy."

Amanda lowered her voice and slowly shook her head. "Unfortunately, something terrible happened back on the houseboat after my client fell asleep on the couch inside. She doesn't know what happened because she was asleep, but she woke up when the police shook her and began questioning her about the bloody knife next to her. The police told her Susan's body was found floating in the water near the houseboat, and Patricia was missing. I concede that it looked bad when the police boarded the houseboat and saw the crime scene. However, there are things that don't add up. For instance, my client and the victim both had marks on their wrists and ankles, proving they both were bound before the police arrived."

Amanda took a step back from the podium and shrugged. "We might not ever know what happened that night on that houseboat, or why. Patricia is missing. I submit that it's possible that she did the killing and set up my client. It's also possible that one of the drunk fishermen from the tournament, who had his advances rejected by the women, followed them to their houseboat and killed Susan, kidnapped Patricia, and set up Lacy. The State doesn't have any proof of what happened, so they are trying to use Facebook posts and texts as evidence. Ladies and gentlemen, don't be fooled by this; we've all typed things when we were angry, posted it online, and regretted it later. Don't allow the prosecutor to use these online rants as something more than what they were."

Amanda stepped forward and held the edge of the podium with her left hand and pointed her right index finger toward Frank. "In conclusion, the burden of proof is on the State, and that burden of proof is beyond all reasonable doubt. There is minimal evidence against my client and he's trying to use Facebook posts and texts to prove this murder. I beg you to listen to my client testify and then compare that to the State's paper-thin evidence. I submit to you that there is so much doubt in this case, you must return a not guilty verdict. Thank you for keeping an open mind during this trial and listening to all of the evidence before you make up your minds."

Chapter 2

Monday, August 17, 2015 at 10:00 a.m.

Courtroom 6B, Lee County Courthouse in Ft. Myers, Florida

The criminal courthouse in downtown Ft. Myers is 10
stories tall and the felony trials are on the six, seventh and
eighth floors of the courthouse, which have side windows
that look out over downtown and the expansive Caloosa-
hatchee River. The trial was taking place in Courtroom 6B
and when you walk into the courtroom from the hallway, the
jury box and jury room is on the right side. The prosecutor's
table was closest to the jury box on the right and the defense
table was on the left side of the courtroom. The witness
stand was to the judge's left, closest to the jury box, and the
clerk sat to the judge's right. The podium for the lawyers to
stand at when questioning the witness was located between
the two tables. There were small wheels on the bottom
of the podium that were used when the bailiffs moved the
podium to face the jury box during opening and closing
statements.

The State Attorney's Office is located on the top four

floors of the SunTrust building in downtown Ft. Myers, adjacent to the courthouse. It's two blocks to the Caloosahatchee River and offers stunning views of the waterfront. Frank's office was on the eighth floor of the SunTrust building, facing northwest toward the river. Beyond the river, he could see North Ft. Myers and Cape Coral on the horizon through his window.

*   *   *   *   *

Frank was dressed in his favorite blue suit, with a crisp white shirt and a red tie for a patriotic flair. He had read many magazine articles, written by psychologists, that stated studies showed that lawyers who wear blue suits in the courtroom are deemed more believable by jurors than lawyers that wear suits of different colors. Frank didn't like clichés, but he didn't like to ignore anything that would help him win a trial, so he always wore "believable blue" on the first day of trial.

In stark contrast, Amanda had chosen to dress in a bright red pant suit with a white silk blouse and black leather four-inch heels. Her outfit was accessorized with a gold butterfly broach with turquoise stones that matched her eyes, and one carat diamond earrings that sparkled brightly because of her unobtrusive pixie haircut. She admired herself in the mirror every morning before she allowed others to observe her believed brilliance.

Amanda had purposefully told Lacy to wear a loose-fitting gray dress, hanging three inches below her knees, with low black pumps and no jewelry. Her sandy blonde hair was pulled back in a pony tail that flowed down about five inches below her shoulders, and she only wore basic make-up. Amanda had personally planned Lacy's bland outfit, hair style, and make-up because she wanted to deemphasize Lacy's natural good looks, and not offend any of the jury because she was wearing jewelry that was nicer than theirs. Lacy didn't like her outfit, or hairstyle, but like Machiavelli she understood - the end justifies the means.

Judge Bronson looked at Frank and said authoritatively, "Mr. Powers, please call your first witness."

Frank turned toward the assistant bailiff standing by the door to the witness room on the side of the courtroom, and said firmly, "As its first witness, the State calls Deputy Bob Simpson."

The assistant bailiff opened the door and motioned for Deputy Simpson to enter the courtroom. A tall uniformed deputy in his mid-thirties entered and approached the clerk's bench. The clerk swore in the deputy, and Judge Bronson asked him to be seated in the witness stand.

"Please give us your name and where you work," Frank said.

"My name is Robert Simpson, but everyone calls me

Bob. I work at the Lee County Sheriff's Office as a marine patrol officer."

"How long have you worked at the Sheriff's department and what jobs have you had since you have been there?"

Deputy Simpson thought for a second. "I've been there a little over 16 years. My first 10 years I was on road patrol, and the last six years I've been on marine patrol."

"Could you tell the jury what the department's marine patrol unit does?"

Deputy Simpson nodded and looked at the jury. "We have 10 deputies that are assigned to our unit and we have four marked sheriff's boats stationed at different marinas throughout the county. We patrol the waters enforcing manatee speed zones and responding to emergencies on the barrier islands and on the water. We also assist the Florida Fish and Wildlife officers and the Coast Guard with anything they request."

Frank nodded. "Let me take you back to May fifteenth of this year. Did you respond to a call at about 3:00 a.m. to a floating body behind Cabbage Key?"

Deputy Simpson sat up in his chair and answered energetically, "I did. My 911 dispatcher called me and said a boater reported a floating body near a houseboat that was anchored southwest of Cabbage Key." Deputy Simpson nodded, took a deep breath, and exhaled. He smiled slightly and continued, "I was actually at home asleep and the phone woke me up. But, I was the duty officer that week for any emergencies that occurred on the water. Because there was a report of a dead body, our protocol was for a road deputy to meet me at Pineland Marina, where my boat was docked, so that we had two deputies responding to the call. I got dressed and drove to the marina in my marked car, with sirens and lights on, and Deputy Arnold was waiting for me at the boat. We drove the boat at high speed, with flashing lights, to the area of the reported body."

"What did you see when you got there?"

Deputy Simson thought for a second before answering. "We came off plane when we got to Cabbage Key and started looking for a houseboat and a floating body on the southwest side of the island. There was a setting moon on the horizon, so it was very dark and our flashing lights created bad conditions for a search. We turned off our flashing lights and turned on our spotlight, and started driving slowly around the reported area of the floating body, near a houseboat anchored on the southwest side of the island. We saw the houseboat anchored about 200 yards from shore."

"Was the good Samaritan boater that made the 911 call still in the area?"

Deputy Simpson shook his head. "No, he told the 911 operator that he didn't want to get involved and didn't leave his name."

"So, what happened next?"

"We drove around the houseboat in a circle looking for the body, but we didn't see anything. We kept going in wider circles, while slowly scanning our spotlight back and forth in the water, until we found the floating body."

Frank pretended to look at his notes to increase the drama, but he was just teasing the jury who wanted the answer immediately. "Where did you find the body?"

Deputy Simpson grimaced and lowered his voice. "We found it about 300 yards south of the houseboat and drove over to it. We called it in to dispatch to confirm the report of a floating body."

Frank could tell his witness was having a hard time. "Do you need a break, officer?"

Deputy Simpson shook his head, took deep breath and sat up in his chair. "No, I'm fine."

Frank gave an understanding nod. "What happened next?"

"We pulled up next to the body and used a docking stick to pull it next to the boat. We then tied ropes around the body and pulled it into the boat."

Frank glanced at the jury, who were all leaning forward on the edge of their seat. "What was the condition of the body?"

Deputy Simpson leaned back in his seat and cleared his throat before he answered. "It was a nude female with a severed neck. Her neck had been cut all the way to her spinal column and the head was hanging forward at about a 45 degree angle, and her red hair was floating wildly in all directions."

Frank glared over at Lacy for a few suspenseful seconds, and she stared blankly back at him. When he looked back at the jurors, he noticed they were also staring at Lacy. He waited a few seconds to allow the jurors to look at the person behind this heinous act before he turned to Deputy Simpson, and asked, "What did you do next?"

"We pulled out a body bag from a storage hatch and secured the body before we approached the houseboat. The body was not bloated, so it hadn't been in the water long, and we were concerned it was possible the murderer was still on the boat. We then pulled our firearms because we didn't know who, or what, we'd find on the houseboat. Deputy Arnold held the spotlight on the houseboat as I drove slowly there."

"What did you see when you tied up to the houseboat?"

Deputy Simpson took a deep breath and wiped his mouth with his sleeve. "We saw blood all on the back deck, but we couldn't see anyone. We shouted to the houseboat and identified ourselves before we boarded. We both had our weapons in the ready position and secured the deck and the roof of the houseboat before we went inside. After that, I opened the back door and Deputy Arnold entered with his flashlight and gun held with both hands in tactical position.

He focused on the Defendant passed out on the couch, as I entered, and saw the bloody knife next to her and kicked it away. While he kept the Defendant lit up, I secured the inside to make sure there was no one else hiding in closets or the bathroom. There was also a smaller boat tied up to the houseboat and I searched it to make sure no one was hiding there, while Deputy Arnold guarded the Defendant."

Again, Frank pretended to look at his notes, but he already knew what he was going to ask because he'd practiced with his witness. "Before you woke up the Defendant, what did she look like?"

"She had blood all over the front of her white blouse and khaki shorts." Deputy Simpson blurted out. "She's laying on her back, with her left leg hanging off the couch and barefooted, kind of like she just passed out."

Frank slowly shook his head. "What did you do next?"

Deputy Simpson exhaled. "I reached down and shook her right arm 'til she woke up. It took a few seconds and she put her hands in front of her eyes, shielding the light, and asking what was going on, but she was acting."

"Objection!" Amanda cried out.

Judge Bronson held up her right hand, with her pointer finger angled towards the ceiling. "Counsel approach." She looked over to the jurors, shook her head and said apologetically, "More white noise while I talk to the lawyers".

Amanda beat Frank and the court reporter to sidebar

with rapid, angry steps. She started to open her mouth, but the judge held up both hands and shook her head. The head bailiff and assistant bailiff moved in like sharks toward a bleeding fish, and Amanda grudgingly stopped her approach because she realized her showmanship was being stopped by the judge. Judge Bronson looked at the head bailiff and gave a slight shake of her head as Frank and the court reporter positioned themselves at sidebar.

Every juror was ready for a confrontation, and at least half of them gave a knowing smile to the judge, eager for an internet moment that they witnessed. One juror secretly wondered how much money she could make with an interview on TMZ.

Judge Bronson brought calm to the storm and said sternly, "Bailiff, take the jury out!"

All the jurors took a disappointed breath and looked toward the head bailiff that had brought them up from the jury room. The head bailiff gave a slight smile and pointed his left hand towards the jury door and slowly nodded.

Judge Bronson stated firmly to the disappointed jurors, "We're going to take a short break and get back with you."

After the jury room door had shut and the head bailiff nodded at Judge Bronson, she looked at Amanda and asked quietly, "What's your objection?"

Amanda thought back to her prior reprimand by the judge and quickly ascertained she needed to be polite and not make speaking objections. "Opinion evidence."

"Sustained." Judge Bronson looked menacingly toward Frank. "Mr. Powers, I respect that a lawyer takes his witnesses to the woodshed and beats some sense into them before they testify. However, if I suspect that a lawyer has coached his witnesses in how to get inadmissible evidence in front of the jury, I'll sanction any lawyer that doesn't follow the rules of the court. Do I make myself clear?"

Everyone in the courtroom was staring at Frank to see how he reacted.

Frank knew he walked a fine line between finding out the truth and coaching a witness to say something that would help him win the case, regardless of the rules of court. He strived to be on the right side of the rules, but sometimes it was a gray, slippery slope and he was convinced he was justified, so he refused to back down.

"Your Honor, my witness responded truthfully when he answered the question, 'What did you do next?'"

Judge Bronson sat back in her chair and gave Frank a smirk while considering his response. After a few seconds of silent deliberation, Judge Bronson said, "Mr. Powers, it's impossible for me to see inside your brain and tell whether or not you improperly coached your witness. However, if your witness makes another remark about the Defendant 'acting', I'll strike him as a witness and instruct the jury to disregard his testimony. Do I make myself clear?"

Frank was angry, but he felt secretly relieved this exchange hadn't occurred in front of the jury. He looked at Judge Bronson and said quietly, "I understand, Your Honor."

Judge Bronson looked at Deputy Simpson and asked loudly, "Do you understand, Deputy?"

"Yes, Your Honor," Deputy Simpson said quietly.

Judge Bronson nodded and looked at the head bailiff. "Bring in the jury."

Everyone resumed their places in the courtroom and Judge Bronson looked at Frank and said sternly, "Please continue your examination."

Frank looked at Deputy Simpson. "After the Defendant asked 'What was going on', what happened next?"

Deputy Simpson responded, "I told her that her friend had her neck sliced open and was dead. She hesitated for a few seconds and then started crying."

"While you were talking to the Defendant, could you smell anything?"

"Oh, yes." Deputy Simpson nodded. "She had a strong smell of alcohol."

Frank looked over at Amanda on the edge of her seat, ready to object to an improper question or answer, and decided to ask an easy question for Deputy Simpson to answer. "What did you do next?"

Deputy Simpson said flatly, "I read her Miranda Rights because I was going to arrest her for murder, no matter what

27

she said."

Frank looked at the judge. "No further questions."

Judge Bronson looked at Amanda. "You may cross examine the witness."

Amanda picked up her yellow note pad and approached the podium as she said, "Thank you, Your Honor."

She set the pad down on the podium, looked up at Deputy Simpson and tightly crossed her arms over her chest. "How many times have you discussed your testimony with the prosecutor before today?"

Deputy Simpson looked uncomfortable and fidgeted in his chair before he answered. "Well, we met last week to talk about the trial. And we met when the case first got sent to his office, and we talked a few times on the phone because we wanted to get everything in line to make sure the trial went smoothly."

"Isn't it true, the first words out of my client's mouth when you woke her up was 'What's going on?'?"

Deputy Simpson shrugged. "Yes, that's what she said."

"After that, isn't it true you told her that Susan had her neck sliced open and was dead?"

The Deputy leaned forward and raised his voice. "Yes, it was pretty obvious she already knew because blood was all over her, and the murder weapon with her fingerprints on it were right next to her."

"Objection, move to strike as non-responsive," Amanda

pleaded.

Judge Bronson leaned forward and glared at Deputy Simpson before she looked towards the head bailiff. "Please take the jury out for a short recess. Deputy Simpson and I need to have a serious discussion."

As the jurors walked toward the jury room, they all avoided eye contact with Deputy Simpson because they sensed Judge Bronson's displeasure. Frank noticed this and wondered how the jury would react to Judge Bronson's reprimand of his witness. Amanda fidgeted at the podium and glared at Deputy Simpson before looking at Judge Bronson hopefully.

After the jury door closed, Judge Bronson folded her arms as she swiveled in her chair to look at Deputy Simpson. "Deputy, my recollection is that you've testified in my courtroom at least a half dozen times over the years, and I've never had a problem with you giving gratuitous comments or opinions before. I realize this is a high pressure trial, with a lot of publicity, and you have your opinion about the Defendant's guilt. However, your opinion does not matter, and in fact, it's against the rules of evidence to give your opinion. Your job is to answer the questions, as completely and accurately as possible, without adding any commentary. Consider this your first and only warning. If you add any of your personal opinions to your future answers, I'll hold you in contempt of court and sentence you to 10 days in jail. Do

I make myself clear?"

Deputy Simpson looked embarrassed and his shoulders slumped before he answered quietly, "Yes, Your Honor."

Judge Bronson looked at the head bailiff and said impatiently, "Bring the jury back in."

After everyone had assumed their places in the courtroom, Amanda looked at Deputy Simpson and gave him an exaggerated smile before she spoke in a saccharine voice. "Deputy, isn't it true my client denied killing Susan?"

"Yes."

"Isn't it true, after she denied killing the victim, you brought her on to your boat, unzipped the body bag, and showed her the victim's severed neck."

Deputy Simpson looked sheepish and looked down before he answered softly, "Yes."

Frank noticed two of the female jurors on the front row raise their eye brows and cross their arms. One older male juror on the back row nodded and glared at the Defendant.

"Deputy Simpson, can you tell me if that is proper protocol at the Lee County Sheriff's Office?"

Deputy Simpson shifted in his seat and took a deep breath. "No, we weren't trained to do that, I just reacted to the situation. I'd never seen someone with their neck cut like that, and I was angry. In hindsight, I would not have done that."

Amanda looked sympathetically over at Lacy before she

turned back to Deputy Simpson. "Isn't it true that my client threw up after seeing her friend's cut neck?"

"Yes."

"Did you continue to question her?"

Deputy Simpson shook his head slowly. "No, Detective Dagle questioned her back at headquarters. I just placed her under arrest and handcuffed her."

Amanda looked at Judge Bronson. "No further questions, Your Honor."

Judge Bronson looked at the witness. "You are excused, Deputy." She then turned to Frank and said, "Please call your next witness."

Frank turned toward the assistant bailiff standing by the door to the witness room on the side of the courtroom, and said firmly, "As its second witness, the State calls Deputy Danny Arnold."

The assistant bailiff opened the door and motioned for Deputy Arnold to enter the courtroom. A skinny uniformed deputy in his mid-forties entered the courtroom and approached the clerk's bench. The clerk swore in the deputy, and Judge Bronson asked him to be seated in the witness stand.

"Please give us your name and where you work." Frank requested.

"My name is Daniel Arnold, but everybody calls me Danny. I work as a Deputy at the Lee County Sheriff's Office."

"How long have you worked there?"

Deputy Arnold cleared his throat. "I've been a deputy for 17 proud years."

Frank nodded and smiled. "Let's go back to May fifteenth of this year. Do you recall where you were that day?"

"I do," Deputy Arnold said and sat up in his chair. "I met Deputy Simpson at Pineland Marina to respond with him to a floating body next to Cabbage Key."

"Did you find a floating body next to Cabbage Key?"

Deputy Arnold looked down and nodded slightly. "We did. Her neck had been sliced open."

Frank waited for Deputy Arnold to look up. "What did you do after you secured the body on the boat?"

Deputy Arnold scratched his chin and looked up before he responded. "We drove over to a houseboat that was nearby and it appeared to be the murder scene."

"Did you and Deputy Simpson find the Defendant on the boat, passed out on a chaise lounge?"

"We did," Deputy Arnold said firmly and shot a nasty glance toward Lacy.

"Was she covered in blood?"

Deputy Arnold nodded. "Yes. We also found a bloody knife on the deck next to her."

"Did Deputy Simpson arrest the Defendant?"

"Yes, he did."

"What did you do after the Defendant was handcuffed and secured?"

"I walked through the houseboat and looked for clues."

Frank looked at his notes momentarily and then looked up at Deputy Arnold. "What did you find in the kitchen of the houseboat?"

Deputy Arnold looked at Lacy and shook his head slowly. "We found two empty glasses, a lime cut in half, a salt shaker, and a half empty bottle of tequila."

Frank looked up at Judge Bronson. "No further questions, Your Honor."

Judge Bronson looked at Amanda. "Do you have any questions, counselor."

"I do, Your Honor," Amanda said as she walked to the podium. Once at the podium, she looked at Deputy Arnold and asked, "Was there any sign of struggle in the kitchen?"

Deputy Arnold slowly shook his head and answered in a bland voice. "No."

Amanda looked at Judge Bronson and announced, "No further questions, Your Honor."

Judge Bronson looked at the jury. "This is a good time to break for lunch. I'll see you back here in one hour. The bailiff will show you out."

Judge Bronson walked off the bench as the head bailiff directed the jurors toward the courtroom door. After the jurors left, everyone who remained in the courtroom relaxed slightly. Frank looked down at this notes and make plans for the afternoon session. He had learned it was best to let the defense lawyer and defendant exit the courthouse before he did. There was nothing more awkward than riding an elevator down with someone you were trying to send away to prison.

Amanda and Lacy gathered their items from the counsel table into their briefcases and purses before they walked out. Frank had asked for a million dollar bond for Lacy, but the judge had only set a $100,000 bond because of Lacy's extensive ties to the community and her lack of criminal record. It bothered him that Lacy was allowed to remain on bond while the case was pending. He couldn't wait until the jury returned a guilty verdict and then Judge Bronson would revoke her bond and sentence her to prison.

Chapter 3

Monday, August 17, 2015 at noon

Lee County Courthouse in Ft. Myers, Florida

As Frank walked out of the courthouse for the lunch break, he enjoyed the fresh air and sunshine during the 100 foot walk to the entrance to the SunTrust building, where the State Attorney's Office was located. People were scurrying to and from both buildings trying to squeeze in lunch, texts, and phone calls before returning to work. Frank greeted his co-workers and friends leaving the building for lunch as he headed toward the elevator. He was meeting the lead detective on the case, Pete Dagle, over a working lunch in his office to discuss his upcoming testimony. As Frank got on the elevator and pushed the eighth floor button, he was pleasantly surprised that he was the only one going up and he closed his eyes, enjoying the silence for the short ride to the eighth floor.

"You made it through the morning with no visible signs of injury," Detective Pete Dagle quipped when Frank got off the elevator.

Pete was five foot, eight inches tall and muscular, but his daily consumption of beer showed on his belly hanging over his belt. He had salt and pepper wavy hair with a handle-bar mustache and dark brown eyes, which made him look like a marshal from an old western movie.

Frank looked wearily at Pete sitting in the reception area. "There were a few skirmishes, but nothing too bad."

Pete stood up and shook Frank's hand. "We've got the evidence; we'll get the conviction no matter what BS that Miami defense lawyer throws out in the courtroom."

"I hope so," Frank said as he pulled out his security card key to access the lobby door and waived at the receptionist behind Plexiglas. Frank opened the door and motioned for Pete to follow him back to his office.

Pete picked up his briefcase and walked toward Frank, "I was following the newspaper reporter's live blog from the courtroom this morning online, and it sounded like the judge was getting a little irritated."

"That's normal for Judge Bronson," Frank lamented as they walked down the hallway to his office.

Frank and Pete said a few hellos and pleasantries to everyone they passed as they walked the 75 feet back to Frank's office. The office, which overlooked the Caloosa-hatchee River, had a worn, over-sized brown Formica topped desk in the middle and two gray metal filing cabinets on the wall to the right of his desk. A small refrigerator sat on top of one of the file cabinets and an old AM/FM radio with a two foot bent antenna on the other. Frank had a well-worn burgundy vinyl swivel chair, and two matching burgundy chairs for his guests on the opposite side of his desk. His college and law school diploma hung on the wall behind his desk chair and the other walls had pinned to them newspaper articles about his trials and thank you letters from victims and police agencies. The one new thing in his office was a modern computer that allowed him quick access to all of the police agencies websites and research links. Pete sat down and admired the view of the river.

Frank walked over to his refrigerator and looked over at Pete. "Do you want a Diet Coke?"

"No, I just had some coffee before I got here."

Frank popped the tab of a Diet Coke and sat down in his chair. "Did you review the trial notebook with all of the Facebook posts and texts between our victim and the Defendant?"

Pete opened up his briefcase and pulled out his notes. "I did. I also did a flow chart with all of the men Lacy and Susan had in common, and it's enough to make even a stripper blush."

Frank laughed as he opened up his desk drawer and pulled out a package of cheese crackers for his lunch. "Those two women dated at least three of the same men over the years and, surprisingly, still stayed friends. My guess is there are more men in common between them that we don't know about."

"They're confirmed peters-in-laws," Pete said sarcastically. "That's why I did the flow chart; I wanted us to have something to refer to during the trial. I reviewed the Defendant's statement and made notes of the dates and the men. If she changes her story on the stand from her statement the night I arrested her, we'll be ready to nail her in front of the jury. I made a copy for you to keep with you at counsel table."

Pete handed the copy to Frank. "Thanks. You never know when you might need this."

Frank's phone chirped with an incoming text. Glancing down at it, he saw the message was from his girlfriend. He held up his finger and said, "Just got a text from Beth. Give me a second."

Pete inclined his head.

The text read: *Hope trial is going good. R we still on for dinner?*

Frank typed in: *Yes, c u @ my place @ 7. Luv u!*

Frank's girlfriend, Beth Mancini, was a local divorce attorney that he had been dating for the past four years. Frank was the happiest he had ever been and most of his friends were intrigued that he had found happiness with a divorce attorney. Some, however, were skeptical and made constant jokes about lawyers finding love together. His favorite was:

What's the best form of birth control for lawyers? Their personality.

"Tell me about the flow chart," Frank said before he put the first cracker in his mouth.

Pete leaned forward in his chair and focused on his copy of the chart on the edge of Frank's desk. "Let's see. In their senior year of college, Lacy's longtime boyfriend knocked Susan up and she had an abortion. Lacy found out about it when they were moving out of their apartment at the end of the year and Susan had left her answering machine in her room. Susan had packed most of her stuff and drove it back to her home in Miami before she came back to Gainesville for graduation. Each of the three roommates all had their own phones in their rooms. Lacy walked by and saw the light was blinking on Susan's phone in her room. She wanted to make sure Susan didn't miss any important messages while she was gone to Miami, so she hit the play button and heard her boyfriend apologizing to Susan about the pregnancy and abortion. After that, the shit hit the fan."

Frank nodded while he ate his cracker lunch and washed it down with Diet Coke.

Pete continued, "A few years after that, in grad school, Lacy started dating one of Susan's old boyfriends from college, and Susan got pissed. Lacy told her karma was a bitch and they didn't talk for a few years. And then, my personal favorite is about 10 years later—Lacy gets divorced from her

39

fireman husband after he gets the seven year itch and cheats with a stripper. The day her ex-husband finds out the judge signed the final divorce decree, he sends Lacy a text saying he'd also been screwing Susan while they were married."

Frank shook his head and asked incredulously, "How in the world did these two women ever stay friends over the years?

Pete smirked and said confidently, "Women are a lot more forgiving than men."

Chapter 4

Monday, August 17, 2015 at 1:05 p.m.

Courtroom 6B, Lee County Courthouse in Ft. Myers, Florida

After everyone had assembled in the courtroom after lunch, Frank looked at the assistant bailiff. "The State calls Dr. Rayner."

The assistant bailiff walked to the witness room, opened the door and motioned for him. Dr. Rayner walked to the front of the courtroom and was sworn in by the clerk. He was dressed in a faded black suit, with a white shirt, and gray tie with a ketchup stain at the bottom. He had a salt and pepper beard that hadn't been trimmed in months and gray hair hanging over his ears. He sat down in the witness stand, leaned forward and faced Frank.

Frank looked at Dr. Rayner. "Please give us your full name and where you work."

Dr. Rayner cleared his throat. "My name is Dr. Alfred Forrest Rayner, IV and I'm the coroner for Lee County, Florida."

"How long have you been a coroner, sir?"

"I was an assistant coroner in Miami right out of medical school for five years, and I've been the head coroner here in Lee County for 21 years."

"Dr. Rayner, do you recall examining the body of Susan Kelly in your office on May fifteenth of this year?"

Dr. Rayner nodded. "I do."

Frank held his hands out to his side in a questioning manner. "What was the condition of the body?"

Dr. Rayner spoke very precisely, as if he were dictating a coroner's report. "The victim was deceased. The body was found in the water, and there was some discoloration of the skin. However, the most dramatic damage to the body was the severed neck. Someone had used a knife and pulled it from the left side of the neck to the right side, cutting the soft tissue all the way through to the top of the spine. The head was hanging forward at about a 45 degree angle. It was definitely a homicide."

"Were there any other unusual injuries to the body?"

Dr. Rayner added. "Yes, there were second degree burns to both nipples and the nostril area. The level of burning was significant, and based on the discoloration of the skin and bruising around the burns, it's my opinion the victim was alive when these areas were burned."

"What is the significance of the victim being alive when these wounds occurred?"

Dr. Rayner leaned towards the microphone and stared

at Lacy as he spoke. "It means the victim appeared to be tortured before she was killed."

Frank glanced at the jury and saw every juror staring at Lacy in disgust. He had planned to ask a few more questions, but decided against it because of the jury's reaction. It was always best to let a defense lawyer ask questions when the jury was focused on the Defendant, and not paying attention to the defense lawyer's questions.

"No further questions, Your Honor."

Judge Bronson looked at the defense table. "Cross examination, Ms. Blayne?"

"Yes, Your Honor," Amanda said as she walked to the podium without any notes.

Dr. Rayner leaned back in his chair, crossed his arm, and focused on Amanda at the podium.

"What is your opinion of how this homicide occurred?" Amanda asked.

Dr. Rayner leaned forward to the microphone. "My opinion is that the killer stood behind the victim, held the victim's head with one hand, and severed the victim's neck with a knife."

Amanda nodded and waited a few seconds before she continued. "Dr. Rayner, isn't it true the entry wound from the knife started at the left side of the neck?"

Dr. Rayner nodded. "Yes."

"Wouldn't you agree with me that the physical evidence

on the neck shows the neck was sliced from the left to the right?"

"I would agree with that."

Amanda raised her hands out to her side. "Wouldn't you also agree that if the killer was standing behind the victim, holding the head with one hand, and slicing the neck with the other, it would stand to reason the killer was right-handed?"

Dr. Rayner pondered the question for a few seconds before he responded cautiously, "I would agree that's a logical inference."

Amanda slowly turned, looking at Lacy writing some notes on a pad and then back at Dr. Rayner. "My client is left-handed, so wouldn't you agree that my client couldn't have killed the victim in the manner you just described?"

Everyone turned and looked at Lacy writing with her left hand. Frank felt a cold sweat forming on his forehead and stood up. "Objection."

Judge Bronson turned her focus from Lacy, who continued writing with her left hand, towards Frank. "Counsel, approach," she said, and then turned toward the jury. "More white noise while we discuss the objection."

Both attorneys approached as the jurors continued to look at Lacy. Once everyone got in position around the bench, Judge Bronson asked, "What's the basis of your objection?"

Frank leaned forward slightly and said in an agitated tone, "Your Honor, this is obviously some staged demonstration the defense lawyer and her client dreamed up to improperly sway the jury."

Amanda leaned forward to speak, but Judge Bronson held up her left hand towards her, and instead spoke to Frank. "Mr. Powers, you still haven't given me the legal basis for your objection. What is it?"

Frank was flustered as he struggled to articulate his objection. After a few seconds and a deep breath, he said, "My objection is that it's an improper question because it calls for a conclusion."

"Objection denied," Judge Bronson said flatly. Judge Bronson gave an irritated side glance toward Amanda and then focused back on Frank. "However, on redirect you can make inquiry of your witness if there is another possibility to explain the fatal injury."

Amanda glared at Judge Bronson for suggesting to Frank a way to minimize the point she'd just made. Judge Bronson returned her glare momentarily before she turned back to Frank and spoke matter-of-factly. "You may resume questioning."

After they returned to their respective places, Amanda looked at Dr. Rayner and asked, "Do you know what type of flame caused the burns to the nipples and nostrils?"

Dr. Rayner shrugged and leaned back as he contemplated his answer. "Any type of cigarette lighter could have caused the damage."

"Are you aware that none of the women on the boat were smokers?"

Dr. Rayner looked uncomfortable as he shook his head. "No, I didn't know that."

"Did you perform toxicology tests on the victim's blood to test for drugs or alcohol?"

"No, I didn't think it was necessary."

Amanda shook her head momentarily before turning toward Judge Bronson. "No further question, Your Honor."

Judge Bronson looked at Frank. "Redirect?"

Frank pulled a binder of his evidence towards him from the front of the table, so he could read it better, and then looked at Judge Bronson. "May I have a moment, Your Honor?"

"You may."

Frank looked at the binder quickly, and then opened a notebook of pictures and pulled one out of the notebook. "May I approach the witness Your Honor?"

"You may."

Frank walked up to Dr. Rayner and put a picture on the sidebar in front of him before stepping to the podium. "Dr. Rayner, I'm showing you State's Exhibit 103. Do your recognize this?"

Dr. Rayner picked up the picture and studied it for a few

seconds before looking up. "I do. This is a picture of the rear deck of the houseboat where the murder occurred."

"Dr. Rayner, do you see a gas grill on the back deck of the houseboat?"

Dr. Rayner nodded. "I do."

"Do you see a lighter on the gas grill's side shelf?"

"Yes, I do," Dr. Rayner said happily.

"Could the lighter for the gas grill have caused the damage to the victim's nipples and nostrils?"

Dr. Rayner nodded and answered enthusiastically, "It most definitely could."

Frank took a deep breath and felt a little better. "Dr. Rayner, is it possible that a left-handed person could have used their dominant hand to hold a struggling victim's head before they sliced their neck?"

Dr. Rayner smiled. "Of course, it's possible."

"No further questions."

Judge Bronson looked at Amanda. "Recross?"

"Yes, Your Honor," Amanda said as she walked rapidly towards the podium with a yellow legal note pad.

Frank noticed that all of the male jurors were admiring Amanda and smiling slightly. The female jurors were all looking at Lacy and had blank faces.

Amanda held up her right hand like she was holding an imaginary baseball. "Dr. Rayner, isn't it true that people use their dominant hand when they throw a ball?"

"Yes, that's true."

Amanda lowered her right hand and acted like she was writing on her yellow legal pad. "Isn't it also true, that people use their dominant hand when they write?"

"Yes, that's also true."

Amanda held up her right hand like she was holding a knife. "Isn't it also true, that when people use a knife to cut their food, they use their dominant hand to hold the knife?"

Dr. Rayner felt himself being boxed in and he didn't like the feeling. He sat back in his chair and said grudgingly, "I suppose this happens, but it's possible someone could use their other hand."

Amanda looked over at the jurors and two female jurors were slowly shaking their heads.

Amanda gave Dr. Rayner an exaggerated smirk and shook her head slowly. "No further questions, Your Honor."

Judge Bronson looked at Frank. "Please call your next witness."

Frank cleared his throat. "The State calls Deputy Ben Hathway."

The bailiff opened the door to the witness room and motioned for him to enter the courtroom. A short, muscular uniformed deputy in his mid-forties entered the courtroom carrying a briefcase and approached the clerk's bench. He had dark brown hair and was cleanly shaved. The clerk swore in the deputy, and Judge Bronson asked him to be seated in the witness stand.

"Please give us your name and where you work." Frank requested.

"My name is Ben Hathway and I work at the Lee County Sheriff's office as a crime scene investigator."

"How long have you been at this job?"

Deputy Hathway thought for a second. "I've been there nine years and three months."

"Let me take you back to May fifteenth of this year. Did you process a murder scene on a houseboat in Pine Island Sound?"

Deputy Hathway nodded. "I did. The houseboat was taken back to Four Winds Marina where it had been rented, and then tied to the dock. The marine deputies put crime scene tape at the base of the dock it was tied to, and around the houseboat, and a guard to preserve the scene until I arrived the next afternoon."

"Why did you get there in the afternoon?"

Deputy Hathway gave a weary look. "I was finishing processing a burglary crime scene at a local high school that had been broken into the night before. I had to finish that before I could start another scene."

Frank gave an understanding nod and continued, "What did you find when you arrived at Four Winds Marina?"

Deputy Hathway glared at Lacy. "I found a houseboat with a bloody back deck and a bloody living room. I took

DNA samples of the blood and sent it all out to the lab. The results showed it all belonged to the victim. The first responders to the crime scene had bagged the knife in an evidence bag. Our fingerprint expert examined it and found the Defendant's fingerprints on the bloody knife, which turned out to be the murder weapon."

Frank turned and pointed towards Lacy. "How did you determine it was the Defendant's fingerprints on the murder weapon?"

"After she was arrested, she was fingerprinted, so we compared those fingerprints to the bloody fingerprints taken from the murder weapon. Our fingerprint expert said it was a perfect forensics match."

There were a few murmurs in the courtroom and Judge Bronson glared at the people making the noise.

Frank waited for the noise to die down. "Deputy Hathway, do you have the murder weapon in your custody?"

"I do," Deputy Hathway pulled it from his briefcase at his feet, secured in a clear plastic evidence bag. "Before court today, I went down to our evidence room and checked it out. It is labeled State's Exhibit Number 1."

Frank looked at Judge Bronson and said dramatically, "I move to introduce the murder weapon into evidence, Your Honor."

Judge Bronson nodded. "It will be received."

Frank walked over to Deputy Hathway and took the

knife in the evidence bag, turned, and walked it over to the clerk's counter. He then looked at Judge Bronson. "No further questions."

Judge Bronson looked over at Amanda. "Does the defense have any questions?"

"I most certainly do," Amanda said gathering her notes. As she walked to the podium, she asked, "Who owned the murder weapon?"

Deputy Hathway cleared his throat and appeared amused by the question. "I assume it was owned by your client because her bloody fingerprints were on it."

Amanda sat her notes on the podium and shook her head. "Not so fast, Deputy Hathway. Surely, as the crime scene investigator in charge, you researched the manufacture stamp on this knife?"

Deputy Hathway sat back in the witness chair and folded his arms in irritation. "Why would I spend tax dollars to research a manufacture stamp on a knife that had the victim's blood and the Defendant's fingerprints?"

Amanda smiled slightly while pulling out an eight inch by eleven inch paper and held it up. "Isn't it true, business records show that this type of knife has only been manufactured for the past two years, and was only sold in Cabela's stores throughout the United States?"

Deputy Hathway shrugged. "I don't know."

Amanda held up a small binder. "Isn't it true, that my

client's credit card and debit card records show that she has never made a purchase in Cabela's stores?"

Deputy Hathway shrugged. "I don't know."

Amanda stared at Deputy Hathway for a few seconds before her next question. "Are you aware that this houseboat was anchored less than a mile from the docks at Cabbage Key when the murder took place?"

"I am."

"Isn't it true that over 100 fishermen were at Cabbage Key the night of the murder for a fishing tournament?"

Deputy Hathway shrugged. "That's what the investigator's report said."

"Isn't it true that fishermen shop at Cabela's stores?"

Deputy Hathway crossed his arms tightly and shrugged. "I guess so."

Amanda held her arms out to her side. "Why didn't you get the credit card records of the fishermen at Cabbage Key to see if they purchased the murder weapon at Cabela's?"

Deputy Hathway leaned forward, obviously irritated. "Again, why would I spend taxpayer's dollars for that when your client's fingerprints were on the murder weapon?"

Amanda pointed at Deputy Hathway and raised her voice. "I would think you'd want to spend taxpayer's dollars to find out who actually purchased the murder weapon, wouldn't you?"

Deputy Hathway sat back in his chair and shook his

head. "I don't know about that."

Amanda held her hands out to her side in frustration. "Don't you think the jury deserves to know the answers to these critical questions?"

Frank jumped to his feet. "Objection, argumentative."

"Sustained," Judge Bronson said sternly as she glared at Amanda.

Amanda looked down at her notes and gathered her thoughts for a few seconds before she continued. She looked up to Deputy Hathway and asked quietly, "What is blood splatter?"

Deputy Hathway considered the question for a few seconds before answering. "Blood splatter is defined as where blood is pushed by force from the body and lands on a solid object. For instance, if a person is standing next to a wall, and is hit by a fist on the face, the angle of the strike and the force determines how much blood is splattered from the nose, against the wall. A second example would be the same person standing by the same wall, but he's shot. The amount of blood that is splattered on the wall is based on the angle of the bullet wound, the caliber of the bullet that goes through the body, and how far away is the shooter from the body."

Amanda nodded slightly before she continued. "How about blood splatter when someone's neck is cut?"

Deputy Hathway quickly answered. "Blood splatter

from a knife wound on an artery creates a very distinctive pattern. When an artery is severed, the blood continues to pump through the artery until the heart stops. It usually takes about two minutes for an adult to bleed out. In the case where a person's carotid artery in the neck is cut, there is a very strong volume of blood that would pump out of the wound, with each heartbeat, until the victim is deceased."

Amanda crossed her arms. "Did you see any evidence of blood splatter on the walls of the houseboat?"

Deputy Hathway finally saw the reason for Amanda's questions and he quickly formulated an answer to help his case. "There's no blood splatter because the victim was facing the water when her neck was cut."

Amanda lifted her hands up and raised her voice. "How do you know that?"

Deputy Hathway smiled smugly. "Because if she wasn't facing the water, blood splatter would be all over the decks and railings of the houseboat."

Amanda put her hands on her hips in exasperation. "Isn't it just as likely that someone else killed the victim, and then mopped up the mess with rags, and squeezed them on my client?"

Deputy Hathway thought for a second. "I suppose that's possible. But how do you explain how the Defendant's fingerprints got on the murder weapon?"

"That is a very good question, Deputy Hathway," Amanda said smugly and smiled. "Is it possible, after the real murderer killed the victim, he wiped his fingerprints from the murder weapon, and then put the knife in Lacy's hand while she was passed out, making her squeeze the knife?"

Deputy Hathway shook his head before he answered sarcastically. "In the words of the church lady from Saturday Night Live, 'isn't that convenient?'"

Amanda snapped her head toward Judge Bronson and pleaded, "Objection, move to strike as non-responsive."

"Sustained," Judge Bronson said firmly.

Amanda hesitated a few seconds and lowered her voice. "Deputy Hathway, weren't there bloody footprints at the crime scene?"

Deputy Hathway said curtly, "There were."

"Did you compare these bloody footprints to the size of the defendant's and victim's feet?"

Deputy Hathway sat back in this chair and crossed his arms. "Of course not. Why would I do that?"

Amanda shook her head in disbelief before she responded. "Isn't it true that if the size of the bloody footprints didn't match the size of the defendant's and victim's feet, then that would mean someone else was there at the bloody crime scene?"

Deputy Hathway shook his head and said firmly, "There was no indication that anyone else was there but your client and the victim."

Amanda looked at the jury, raised her eyebrows, and shook her head in irritation. After a few moments, she turned to Deputy Hathway and said sarcastically, "I guess we'll never know for sure because you didn't do your job, did you?"

"Objection. That's an argumentative question." Frank said angrily as he stood up.

"Sustained." Judge Bronson said flatly and gave Amanda a nasty stare.

Amanda looked at the bewildered jury and smiled. "No further questions."

Judge Bronson cleared her throat and looked at the jury. "It's late in the day, so we're going to recess for the day. I'll see you tomorrow morning at 9:00 a.m. sharp."

Chapter 5

Monday, August 17, 2015 at 6:00 p.m.

Frank Power's condo in Ft. Myers, Florida

Frank owned a condominium on the tenth floor of the
Downtown Towers complex, looking over the Caloosa-
hatchee River, which was about a mile wide there and flowed
west, emptying into the Gulf of Mexico by Sanibel Island.
Frank's condo was a two bedroom with two baths and had
two dedicated parking spots in the gated parking garage on
the second level. There was a large swimming pool and club
house on the third level that was popular with the residents.
Each unit had a 10-foot closet by its parking spaces for storage. Frank kept his bike there and religiously rode it five
miles every morning before work.

After Frank got home from the trial for the day, he
poured himself a scotch and started making dinner for Beth
in his classic bachelor style. He'd discovered early in their
relationship that she liked Marie Callender's frozen chicken
alfredo dinners, so he always had a few in the freezer for
quiet and relaxed stay-at-home dinners with Beth. He pulled

one out and pre-heated his oven before he began chopping up vegetables for salad. After he finished making their salads, he put the two bowls in the refrigerator and the frozen dinner in the oven. He refilled his scotch, added some ice, and walked out to his lanai to watch the sun set as he waited for Beth to join him.

When Frank was 12, his father was convicted of trafficking in cocaine and sentenced to 30 years in prison because of his two prior drug convictions. One year after Frank's father went to prison, his mother married the defense lawyer that had represented his father. She had assured Frank the romance only started after Frank's dad went away, but he harbored lingering doubts and hated his step-father. When Frank was 17, his step-father died of a heart attack, and his mom collected on the one million dollar life insurance policy.

Three months later, Frank's mom met a slick yacht salesman in West Palm Beach. He wined her and dined her and took her to Las Vegas six weeks into the relationship. After a passionate weekend, he proposed and they married at a drive-through chapel two hours later. Within two years, the money was gone and Frank's second step-father divorced his mother. His mother then lost her house due to foreclosure and moved to a trailer park, which was where she met her fourth husband. During the rocky marriage, he had been arrested four times for domestic violence against her, but

Frank's mother always dropped the charges and took him back. Frank only saw his mother when her husband wasn't with her, because he knew he might beat him senseless, and then his co-workers would have to prosecute him.

When Frank's father was released from prison, he met Frank once for lunch. The lunch only lasted 45 minutes and the conversation was minimal, with both of them shifting uncomfortably in their chairs and avoiding eye contact. Frank's father became irritated at the end of the lunch, stood up, put a $50 bill on the table and walked away, without a handshake or a goodbye. After that, he moved to Columbia, South America and hadn't been heard from since. Because of his parents' bad luck with marriage, and Frank's dedication to his career, he'd never married or had any children.

* * * * *

Beth was a young-looking 48 year-old in pretty good shape, but no one had ever called her beautiful. She always had fruit for breakfast and salads for lunch, but her creamy pasta addiction was her major downfall for dinners. She power-walked five days a week for two miles around her neighborhood with pink rubber barbells and ankle weights. She walked the stairs to her third floor office daily, but she couldn't shed the 25 pounds she'd been trying to lose for 15 years. She dyed her hair the shade of brown closest to her natural color to keep out the approaching gray. When she was younger, she had stayed out of the sun so now her fair skin was aging better than all of the tanning salon queens she'd grown up with. She got her teeth brightened every year and was often told her smile was her best trait. One of her biggest embarrassments was that she was a reformed nail biter, but times of stress caused her to have occasional relapses resulting in a quick trip to the salon for fake nails to cover the evidence of her binge biting.

Frank's condo was about half way between Beth's office and her home in Edison Park, so it was a five minute drive for Beth either way.

Edison Park had wide curving streets, tall trees and lush vegetation. It was adjacent to Thomas Edison's historic winter home and laboratory on the Caloosahatchee River. In Edison's will, he had donated his property to the City of Ft. Myers for a museum, and it had been a popular tourist destination since then. The surrounding houses in Edison Park were an eclectic mix of old Spanish, modern ranch and old Florida with tin roofs and brick fireplaces. There existed a mixture of young families, retirees and childless middle-age professionals like her, but everyone was friendly and participated in the neighborhood watch program to keep out crime.

Beth's home was an old Spanish style house built in 1925, with three bedrooms and two baths. It had a rough stucco finish, painted dark tan with a red tile roof and a curved mahogany door. There were old Florida wide planked pine wood floors throughout the house, except for the tiled bathrooms. The dining room had cypress paneling on the walls and there were high ceilings with deep crown molding in every room. There was a gazebo in the back yard that was next to a fire pit that Beth used during the winter months. Her St. Augustine grass was deeply fertilized and perfectly manicured. Beth was very proud of all the work she'd done since she bought the house and fixed it up.

Frank had given her a gate remote and a resident's sticker for her five-year-old white Toyota Camry. She had gone home after work and taken a cool shower to refresh from the summer humidity. She'd dressed in a pink cotton sun dress and pink flip flops for the short drive to Frank's condo, but she knew after dinner she'd put on Frank's favorite outfit for her – one of his white t-shirts and nothing else.

Beth walked in her kitchen door and her two cats, a Persian named Bella and a Tabby named Gracie, greeted her with loud meows as they rubbed against her legs. They were typical cats—if Beth was home they'd hide under the bed or in other rooms, but if she spent the night at Frank's condo, they complained loudly when she returned. She had water and food canisters that automatically filled up the bowls, so they never suffered when she wasn't home. Beth decided she needed to give them some love before she left, so she picked them up and held them to her chest as she kissed them. They both purred loudly and gently rubbed their chins on Beth's neck. After a few minutes of mutual love, she set them down and they walked away, seemingly disinterested.

Beth locked up her house and walked outside toward her Camry. She saw a big summer thunderstorm blowing in from the east and estimated it would be at Frank's condo in about 15 minutes. By that time, she'd have a glass of Merlot in hand and would be watching it safely in Frank's condo.

*   *   *   *   *

"Hello, lover," Beth said happily as Frank opened up his front door.

Frank smiled as he stepped forward and pulled her close. "You're the best thing I've seen all day," he said before he kissed her.

Beth felt a tingle in her neck as she kissed his warm lips and pulled him close. After a few seconds of kissing, she slowly pulled her lips away and purred, "What's a girl got to do to get a drink around here?"

Frank smiled. "I have a bottle of Merlot out and vodka, but I wasn't sure what your mood was tonight. What would you like?"

Thunder rolled in the distance and Beth answered sweetly, "Honey, a nice tall glass of Merlot would be divine."

Frank led the way to the kitchen and opened the bottle of

Merlot. Beth feigned surprise as she sniffed the air, "Oh my, what could that delicious smell be coming from your oven?"

Frank poured the Merlot and played along. "It's this newest version of wheat pasta, with just a touch of marinara sauce, and fat-free turkey sausage I found in the organic frozen food section at the grocery store."

Beth rolled her eyes and shook her head. "You always cook my favorite, and it shows on my hips."

Frank handed her the wine glass. "I guess we'll just have to work it off, later."

"We always do, honey." Beth smiled coyly and took a sip.

Frank pointed out at the lanai. "Let's go relax and watch the storm cross the river."

She nodded and followed him out to the table on the lanai. They sat down and enjoyed their drinks as they watched a dark storm line cross the river and felt the wind increase as the temperature dropped. During the summer months, the humidity-driven thunderstorms came almost daily in the late afternoon or early evening, and helped make the summer heat ease off and life more bearable. From their tenth floor vantage point, Frank and Beth had a bird's eye view of the lightning strikes and felt the full force of thunder claps. After about five minutes of the noisy aerial show, the storm line passed behind the condo and a steady rain began as the temperature continued to drop. With the fading sunlight and steady rain, all of the colors outside were either grays or light blue.

"So how'd the trial go today?" Beth asked.

Frank drained his scotch and nodded. "So far, no surprises with the witnesses. The defense lawyer thoroughly lived up to her reputation of pushing the limits with judges. Judge Bronson calmed her down, but she's always trying her best to say things to get you distracted. Of course, she knows how the game is played because she used to be a prosecutor. It always pisses me off when a prosecutor quits our office, and goes to the dark side, and then uses the knowledge of our office against us."

"Have you ever met her before this case?" Beth asked as she leaned back in her chair.

Frank shook his head. "I'd never met her, but I called a couple of my law school buddies in Miami and they gave me the low down on her. She knows how to focus on the weak parts of your case, and she prides herself in trying to get under your skin and make you look bad in front of the jury. She's won every trial she has had since she became a defense lawyer. Her real talent though is that the jurors love her—my opinion is the women like her smarts and the men like her looks."

"Men are very simple creatures," Beth quipped and took a drink of her wine.

Frank nodded and smiled wearily. The stressful trial had

drained his energy.

Beth had represented the missing woman, Patricia Hendricks, in her messy divorce case. Patricia's ex-husband, David Brennen, was a jeweler and a trust fund baby. He'd been violent with her in the past and they'd separated and reconciled many times before she finally found the courage to file for divorce. The case lasted for two years because he did everything to delay the case and try to convince her to reconcile. He'd never signed any divorce agreement stating the marriage was irretrievably broken, because he wanted to desperately reconcile. Since he wouldn't agree to the divorce, they had to go to trial to get a judge to rule that the marriage was, in fact, irretrievably broken. The judge finally signed the divorce decree three months before the houseboat trip.

"What did the defense lawyer say about Patricia's disappearance?"

Frank shook his head slowly. "She suggested that Patricia could have killed Susan and set up Lacy."

"That bitch! Patricia never could've done anything like that."

Frank held up his hands in mock self-defense. "I know she couldn't do anything like that, but a defense lawyer's job is to try and create reasonable doubt. She also suggested that another alternative is some drunk fisherman from Cabbage Key followed them back to their boat because he got mad when the women turned him down, and embarrassed him in front of friends, so he wanted revenge."

Beth shook her right pointer finger at Frank and said irritably, "That's a bunch of bullshit! They found the bloody knife with Lacy's fingerprints on it next to her body. She'd threatened to kill Susan in the past on Facebook and in texts. She got drunk and attacked Susan, Patricia tried to stop it, and Lacy killed her too. I don't know if the sharks ate Patricia's body, or if the tide took it out to sea, but she's dead too. Amanda can try to spin it whatever way she wants, but anybody with a brain can see she's guilty as sin!"

Frank nodded and said sympathetically, "I wish you were on my jury!"

Beth shook her head in frustration and closed her eyes tight as she thought of her former client's body being eaten by sharks. Her obsessive compulsive disorder kicked in and she started debating with herself if it was one huge shark that ate her client in two bites, or a school of sharks ripping her body in shreds, slowly and methodically. After a few seconds of her mental gymnastics, she opened her eyes, drained her wine glass, and banished the gruesome thoughts from her mind.

Beth held her glass out to Frank, smiling sweetly, "A refill, please?"

Frank wasn't sure what Beth was thinking when her eyes were closed, but he was certain from her demeanor he shouldn't ask, so he took her glass and dutifully walked towards the kitchen for a refill. He left the lanai slider open as he walked in and changed the subject by asking, "How are Bella and Gracie doing?"

Beth gushed, "They're my loves. I wish you weren't allergic to cats so you'd come over and play with them."

"I love cats, but you know I can't be around them," Frank lamented as he poured her wine.

Beth watched the colors of the sunset change as the storm blew over and thought of how good her life was in Ft. Myers. She had a rewarding job helping her clients through divorces, and she made a good living at the same time. She'd been in her relationship with Frank for four years, and every day she grew closer to him. They both said they weren't interested in marriage, but they'd both admitted they enjoyed being committed to each other and, at this point in Beth's life, that was all she really wanted.

Frank walked back on the lanai and handed Beth her glass. "I wish we had pets we could share together."

Beth cocked her head. "Really?"

Frank nodded. "During law school, my mother gave me a Jack Russell as a Christmas gift and it was the greatest gift I'd ever gotten. I named him Buddy." Frank sat down and took a heavy drink of his scotch and breathed out heavily. "At least for six months before he broke my heart."

Beth sat up in her chair. "You never told me about that."

Franked smiled wistfully and drained his scotch. He felt his eyes start to tear up as he said in a wavering voice, "I took him in to the vet because he had a growth on his back right foot and was yelping every time he walked up the steps to my apartment. The vet found a tumor and told me it was incurable cancer. He'd be dead in 45-60 days, no matter what we did. She recommended I put him down because his pain would increase every day until he died."

Beth felt her neck stiffen and a cold shiver ran down her spine. "What did you do?" she whispered.

Frank took a deep breath and stood up. He walked toward the screen and faced the sunset, "I thought about it for a few minutes, and I knew what I had to do because I loved him."

Beth slowly walked over and stood behind Frank, putting her arms around his ribs and squeezed his belly. She felt his lungs fill up with air and heard him start to cry for the first time ever in their relationship. She held him tighter, and Frank put his hands over hers and allowed himself to cry.

A minute later Frank wiped his tears away, turned, and pulled Beth toward him. He whispered, "I was sitting on the ground and holding Buddy when they injected him with the sleep agent. I felt his body relax and helped him lay down for the last time. After a few seconds, I nodded at the vet and she gave him the final dose. I held him until I couldn't feel his heart beat any more and then I cried uncontrollably for a while."

Frank sobbed as he held Beth for a minute before he said sadly, "When I walked out of the vet's office that night, I swore to myself that I'd never have a dog again because it hurt so badly to put him down. It's been 28 years and I haven't had a dog since."

Beth had tears in her eyes and pulled Frank close and squeezed as she laid her head gently on his chest. She was a little surprised, she'd rarely seen Frank's sentimental side before, but she was happy he'd shared it with her.

After a few seconds of silence, he squeezed her tightly back and whispered in her left ear, "I'd get a dog with you, if you wanted."

Chapter 6

Tuesday, August 18, 2015 at 9:02 a.m.

Courtroom 6B, Lee County Courthouse in Ft. Myers, Florida

"Good morning, ladies and gentlemen of the jury," Judge Bronson said cheerily, opening the day of trial. She then looked at Frank. "Please call your next witness."

Frank looked at the assistant bailiff. "The State calls Rod Gladding."

The assistant bailiff walked to the witness room, opened the door and motioned for the witness. Rod Gladding walked to the front of the courtroom and was sworn in by the clerk. He was in his mid-thirties, about 5'9", tanned, trim and dressed in a foam green Columbia fishing shirt with jeans and faded topsiders. As he walked to the witness stand, all of the woman in the jury admired his physique. He sat down in the witness stand, leaned forward and faced Frank.

"Please give us your name and place of employment," Franks said pleasantly.

Rod answered in a deep voice, "My name is Rod Gladding, and I work as a fork lift operator and rental boat manager at Four Winds Marina in Bokeelia."

"How do we get to Four Winds Marina from downtown Ft. Myers?" Frank asked cordially.

"You go north on U.S. 41 until you hit Pine Island Road. Make a left and stay on it for about 15 miles. You go through Cape Coral and the old fishing village of Matlacha until you come to a four-way stop on Pine Island. After that, make a right and go about six miles to the north end of Pine Island, and Four Winds Marina is on the left. The marina basin is on Jug Creek and it empties out into Pine Island Sound."

Frank took a deep breath and changed to a serious tone. "Do you know a woman named Patricia Hendricks?"

Rod smiled and nodded. "I do. She's been keeping her 19-foot Boston Whaler at the marina for a few years. It's still at the marina in storage. The Sheriff's department brought it back to the marina after what happened on the houseboat."

"When did you see her last?"

Rod took a deep breath and cocked his head as he pondered his answer. "The last time I saw her was a weekend in mid-May of this year when she rented the 30-foot houseboat from our marina with her two friends. They left the marina with her smaller boat being towed behind the houseboat." He shook his head slowly. "I haven't seen her since."

Frank held his hands to his side in a questioning manner. "Could you describe to me how she was acting with her two friends at the marina the last time you saw her?"

Rod leaned back and considered his words before he answered. "It was quite interesting when they all showed up. We're all kinda used to Patricia wearing long pants, long sleeved shirts and big hats because she's so fair skinned and didn't want to get sunburned. She normally shows up with friends that're dressed the same way to go fishin' in her boat. But this time, her friends were dressed very differently— they both had on skimpy bikinis and were ready to party. One was a tall thin blonde and the other was a shorter, curvy red head. They were both drinking margaritas and flirting with all of the guys at the marina."

"What do you mean by flirting?"

Rod blushed. "They were going around the marina and hugging the guys and invitin' us to meet them later at Cabbage Key for drinks."

There were a few snickers in the courtroom and Frank let it quiet down before he continued. "Was Patricia drinking margaritas?"

Rod looked up to his left and thought for a second. "I remember her drinking bottled water. I guess she was the designated driver."

"Did you ever observe any disagreements between the women in the bikinis?"

Rod nodded. "I did. The tall blonde had her arm around me and was talking to me for a few minutes, and then she went to the bathroom. While she was gone, the red head came over and started flirting. The next thing I know she's hugging me and gives me a wet kiss. That's when I hear the blonde yell out across the marina, 'He's mine!' They start yelling at each other, and everybody in the marina stopped what they were doing and looked at the three of us. I was a little embarrassed."

Frank nodded and waited for a few moments before he asked, "What happened next?"

"Patricia came over and stood between them while they were arguing and tried to keep the peace—it was quite the show."

"Did the blonde say something that made you think there was a bad history between the two women?"

Rod chewed on his bottom lip for a second and said hesitantly, "The blonde said 'Haven't you taken enough of my men?'"

Frank waited for a few moments to let the jury focus on the answer, and then asked politely, "What happened next?"

Rod shrugged. "The argument kinda simmered down, and I helped them load their supplies and luggage on the houseboat."

"What were they doing the last time you saw them that day?"

Rod smiled. "They were all on the top deck of the houseboat as Patricia drove it out of the marina, drinking and dancing to Jimmy Buffett music. I think the song was 'Cheeseburger in Paradise.'"

Frank looked at Judge Bronson. "No further questions."

Judge Bronson glanced at Amanda. "Cross-examination?"

Amanda walked to the podium, turned to Rod, and asked politely, "How long did the argument last between the blonde and redhead?"

Rod shrugged his shoulders. "Just a few minutes."

Amanda held her hands out to her side and asked matter-of-factly, "After this short spat, did the girls go back to being in a good mood?"

Rod nodded. "They did. They were ready to party, no doubt about that."

"In fact, didn't the two girls in the bikinis hug each other after their spat?"

Rod leaned back in chair and blushed. "They did and then they both blew a kiss towards me while they were hugging each other and giggled."

Two of the male jurors in the back row looked at each other and smiled slightly.

Amanda gave him a mischievous smile and said slyly, "No further questions, Rod."

Judge Bronson dismissed Rod and then looked at Frank.

"Your next witness?"

Frank looked at the assistant bailiff. "The State calls Claudia Volk."

Rod walked out of the courtroom as the assistant bailiff walked to the witness room, opened the door, and motioned for the next witness. Claudia walked to the front of the courtroom and was sworn in by the clerk. She was an attractive, middle-aged lady with natural blonde hair that hung just above her shoulders. She was dressed in a turquoise blouse and white skirt with white pumps. She sat down in the witness stand, faced Frank and smiled.

"Please give us your name and where you work."

"My name is Claudia Volk, and I work as the manager at Cabbage Key."

"How long have you worked at Cabbage Key?"

"Eight wonderful years."

"Could you tell the jury what Cabbage Key is and its history?"

Claudia beamed and nodded. "It's a small island resort about 15 minutes by boat from the north end of Pine Island. The restaurant and bar is built on top of an old Indian mound, and at 38 feet, it's the highest point in all of Lee County. In 1944, the owners built a rustic fishing resort with six rental rooms and seven rental cottages and a marina with overnight dockage for yachts. In 1976, the current owners, Rob and Phyllis Wells, bought it and upgraded it. In 2004, the eye of Hurricane Charlie passed over it with 147 mile an hour winds, but it survived and was rebuilt. People come from all over the world to enjoy our little slice of paradise."

Frank smiled politely and asked, "Isn't that the island restaurant with all of the signed dollar bills taped to the walls?"

"Yes. It's an old tradition that started over seventy years ago when the resort opened," Claudia smiled. "There were more commercial fishermen than tourists back then. Of course, when the fishermen had good days, they had plenty of cash for beer. On bad fishing days, they were broke and thirsty. One smart fisherman taped a dollar bill to the wall with his name on it, so he'd always have cash for a drink. The tourists saw it and started doing it for fun. Pretty soon, the walls were covered in dollar bills."

Frank glanced at his notes for a second and then back at Claudia. "Let me take you back to May fifteenth of this year. Was there a fishing tournament at Cabbage Key that weekend?"

Claudia nodded. "We had the annual 'Big Snook Invitational Tournament' going on with about 100 anglers staying on the island, or in docked yachts at the marina. It's our biggest tournament of the year and we always have a big turnout of the best fishermen in the area. It's a very competitive event and everyone at that tournament is so much fun."

Frank cocked his head to his left. "Were most of these

anglers men?"

Claudia touched a finger to her lips momentarily as she calculated. "It was probably about 80 percent men. However, the biggest snook in the tournament was caught by a woman."

Two of the female jurors nodded in approval.

Frank cleared his throat and asked, "Do you recall three ladies that weren't in the tournament who showed up at the bar after the Captain's meeting was over?"

Claudia smiled. "I do. One of our regulars is Patricia Hendricks, and she arrived with two of her friends—a blonde named Lacy and a redhead named Susan. They created quite the scene because they were very pretty and dressed quite provocatively."

"How were the three women acting towards each other?"

Claudia took a deep breath and leaned back in her chair. "At first, they were having a ball, drinking and flirting with all of the men. They all seemed to be enjoying the attention. We had the music playing in the bar and some of the guys asked them to dance. Once they got on the dance floor, it seemed like they were in competition with each other to see who could get the most attention."

"What happened later?"

Claudia shrugged. "I was busy working, so I don't know all of the details, but towards closing time, I heard an argument break out in the bar between two women. I walked into the bar and Lacy and Susan were yelling at each other. Patricia was standing between them trying to calm them down."

"Do you recall any part of the argument that stands out?"

Claudia cocked her head and looked up before she answered, "I remember Lacy yelling about Susan always taking her men. After that, Susan was flustered and walked outside, while Lacy went to the bar and did a shot of tequila."

"Do you remember seeing how they left the island?"

Claudia nodded. "I was concerned that two of the three women were obviously very drunk, and I didn't want anyone to fall and hurt themselves. So, I followed them down to the dock and saw them all get on a boat. Patricia, who appeared to be sober, was driving the boat, so I was relieved. She told me they were staying on a houseboat on the other side of the island. At that point, I figured they were fine, so I went back to the restaurant and finished my shift."

Frank looked at Judge Bronson. "No further questions."

Judge Bronson glanced at Amanda. "Cross examination?"

Amanda walked toward the podium and said sweetly, "Thank you, Your Honor."

Judge Bronson looked suspiciously toward Amanda.

After Amanda got situated at the podium with her notes, she looked up at Claudia. "Isn't it true that when the three women arrived at the bar, they were on good terms?"

Claudia nodded. "Yes, they were all smiling and having fun."

"Isn't it true, that when they left the bar, they were on good terms?"

Claudia shrugged. "They seemed to be after the argument was over and they'd calmed down a little bit. They were telling all of the fishermen they'd be back tomorrow to party with them. They all walked down to their boat together in seemingly good spirits."

Amanda nodded slowly and looked at Judge Bronson. "No further questions, Your Honor."

Judge Bronson looked at the jury. "This is a good time to break for lunch. I'll see you back in an hour."

Chapter 7

Judge Alexandra Lynn Bronson was born and raised in Sarasota, Florida. She was the older of two daughters, born to a single mom that worked her entire life as a maid until killed by a drunk driver at age 52. Judge Bronson's sister, Beth-Anne, was eight months pregnant when their mother died, so she decided to honor her mother's memory by naming her daughter after her. Judge Bronson was holding her sister's hand when baby Claire entered the world. Claire's father was not there for her birth, or anytime thereafter.

Judge Bronson received an academic scholarship to the University of North Carolina and graduated with a degree in history. She decided to be an academic rebel and attend law school at Duke, her undergraduate school's long-time rival. While at law school at Duke, she met and fell in love with her future husband, Peter Schilling, a medical student. Peter was from Ft. Myers, Florida and they moved back to his home and married after they finished their education.

81

Judge Bronson was a young public defender and Dr. Schilling was an internist in Ft. Myers, and they seemed to have the perfect life ahead of them. Everyone in town considered them to be a power couple and would prosper together. However, after Judge Bronson had two miscarriages in their first three years of marriage, Dr. Schilling decided to end their marriage and started dating his nurse. The divorce took six months to finalize and the nurse was pregnant by the time the divorce was final. Dr. Schilling married his nurse the day after the divorce was final and the baby was born three months later.

Judge Bronson was devastated by her husband's lack of commitment with her and trading her in for a younger, more fertile woman. She channeled her anger into her career and began volunteering to take the hardest cases at the Public Defender's office. Many of her cases went to trial, and her trial skills allowed most of her clients to walk out of the courtroom innocent citizens because of not guilty verdicts.

In her seventh year as a public defender, she had the biggest trial of her career. A 30 year old mother of two was charged with second degree murder for shooting her husband 12 times after he slapped her in their home. He'd come home at midnight after a night of drinking at the local bar and she'd confronted him about it in their bedroom. After he slapped her, she pulled a .38 revolver out of the night-stand, shot him, and kept firing until she was out of bullets, reloaded, and emptied the gun again into his lifeless body. Every news outlet broadcasted the sensational murder and the public's fascination with the killing guaranteed continued news coverage through the trial.

After the wife was arrested, the public defender's office was appointed to represent her and Judge Bronson was assigned the case. During her investigation of the case, it was discovered that the wife had been a long-time victim of domestic violence during the marriage. Her husband had been arrested twice for domestic violence during the marriage, and the wife had been taken to the hospital six times during the marriage because of domestic abuse. Judge Bronson hired a psychologist that specialized in domestic violence cases to testify as a defense expert at trial. She testified that the wife was in actual fear of more severe abuse than the slapping because of her history of abuse during the marriage. The jury agreed with the expert as well as with Judge Bronson's self-defense argument, and acquitted the wife of the charges.

After the trial, every law firm in town took notice of Judge Bronson's trial skills, and she had three lucrative job offers within a week of the verdict. She took the highest paying offer from a firm that specialized in insurance defense cases. For the next eight years, she won many personal injury trials for the insurance companies she represented, and saved all of her bonus checks for retirement. At age 40, the governor appointed her circuit judge and she has been on the bench for the past 20 years handling criminal trials in Ft. Myers.

Judge Bronson's favorite hobby was spoiling her niece, Claire, who lived in Sarasota. Judge Bronson never tried to have children after her miscarriages, and her sister had a hysterectomy shortly after Claire was born and couldn't conceive any other children. Claire was Judge Bronson's only blood relative and she happily paid for private schools and any activity that Claire desired. Judge Bronson was certain her mother would have approved.

Chapter 8

Tuesday, August 18, 2015 at 1:05 p.m.

Courtroom 6B, Lee County Courthouse in Ft. Myers, Florida

Judge Bronson addressed the jurors, "Ladies and gentlemen, I hope you had a good lunch." She then looked at Frank, "Please call your next witness."

Frank looked at the assistant bailiff. "The State calls Detective Pete Dagle."

The assistant bailiff walked to the witness room, opened the door, and motioned with his finger. Detective Dagle walked to the front of the courtroom and was sworn in by the clerk. He sat down in the witness stand and faced Frank.

Frank asked, "What's your name?"

"My name is Pete Erwin Dagle."

"Where do you work and what's your job?"

"I'm a Detective with the Lee County Sheriff's Office."

"How long have you worked with the Sheriff's Office?"

"I've been there 20 years. My first nine years, I was a road deputy. I was promoted to detective after that."

"How were you involved in this case?"

Pete looked at the jury and explained in an authoritative voice, "After the responding deputies realized it was a homicide case, the detective division was notified. Since I was the detective available that night, the case was assigned to me."

"When did you receive a call about this case, and what did you then do?"

"My phone rang at 5:30 a.m. and woke me up with the news of the homicide and that they had arrested a suspect, Lacy Turner. I advised the responding deputy to bring her to the interview room at the Sheriff's Department on Six Mile Cypress Parkway, and I'd meet them there for a videotaped interview."

"When did you interview the Defendant, Lacy Turner?"

Detective Dagle looked down at his notes before he answered. "They had to transport the suspect by boat to Pineland Marina, and then drive her to headquarters in a marked cruiser, so it took a few hours. My notes show that the date-stamped time on the beginning of the video interview was at 7:38 a.m."

"Do you have a digital recording of that interview on your laptop, and if so, have you reviewed it for accuracy?"

Detective Dagle nodded. "I have the digital recording and it's an accurate recording of the interview I did that morning. I have downloaded a copy to your laptop, and it's an accurate copy."

Frank looked at Judge Bronson. "Your Honor, I'd like to

move this video into evidence and publish it for the jury."

Judge Bronson looked over at Amanda. "Any objections?"

Amanda stood and shook her head. "No, Your Honor"

"The video is admitted, without objection." Judge Bronson nodded at Amanda and then looked at the jury. "Ladies and gentleman of the jury, the video of the interview has been admitted into evidence, and the prosecutor's laptop is hooked up to this courtroom's large screen mounted on the wall across from you. At this time, the entire interview will be played for you, and should be considered by you in your deliberations."

Judge Bronson turned and nodded at Frank, who hit the play function on his laptop, while the assistant bailiff lowered the lights in the courtroom. Everyone in the courtroom focused on the large screen as the interview began. The ceiling camera in the interview room at the Sheriff's Office was in the back corner of a 10 foot by 10 foot, cream colored room, with a small wood table in the middle, a box of Kleenex in the middle of the table, along with a dirty ashtray and two metal chairs on each opposite side. The front of Lacy's face and the back of Detective Dagle's head were visible as the interview tape started.

Detective Dagle began the interview. "Ms. Turner, I need to read you your Miranda rights before we begin the interview. You have the right to remain silent. Anything you say can and will be used against you in a court of law. You have the right to an attorney. If you cannot afford an attorney, one will be provided for you. Do you understand the rights I have just read to you?"

Lacy nodded and spoke softly. "Yes."

"With these rights in mind, do you wish to speak to me?"

"I do." Lacy sat up in her chair and pleaded, "I don't remember what happened, but I know that I didn't kill Susan."

Lacy's blonde hair was disheveled, and even though her face and hands had been washed clean, after the transport officer brought her in from Pineland Marina, her white blouse still showed blood splatter.

Detective Dagle was a skilled interviewer and used a sympathetic tone to begin the interview. "I understand. My job is to find out what you remember and get the truth out for everyone to see."

Lacy nodded emphatically. "That's what I want too."

Detective Dagle looked down at his notes for a moment. "Let's start with all three of you ladies driving to Four Winds Marina to rent the houseboat. What was the reason you decided to rent a houseboat and anchor behind Cabbage Key for the weekend?"

Lacy took a deep breath before she began. "All of us have been friends since college, and we'd all gotten divorced in the past year, so we decided to have a girls' weekend. Patricia kept her 19-foot boat at the marina, and knew about a houseboat that they rented out there. I knew that some of my buddies were fishing in a snook tournament at Cabbage Key for the weekend, so we decided it'd be fun to go over there and look for guys to party with us."

"When did you go over to Cabbage Key, and how'd you get there?"

"We towed Patricia's boat behind the houseboat to a quiet cove behind Cabbage Key. We left the houseboat anchored there, and drove Patricia's boat to the Cabbage Key dock around sunset, so we probably got there around eight last night."

Detective Dagle wrote a few notes on his pad before he looked up. "What happened when you got to Cabbage Key?"

Lacy shrugged. "We were in the right place for fun—a lot of good-looking fishermen that were partying hard and very few other women. We had men buying us drinks and hitting on us as soon as we walked in the bar. We danced a little bit and I was talking to a bunch of my friends. A guy I used to date casually came up and started flirting with me, and I was enjoying talking with him. Well, I went to the bathroom, and when I came back, I saw Susan talking with him, and I got my feelings hurt. I told Patricia I wanted to leave, so she gathered up Susan and we came back to the houseboat."

Detective Dagle scratched his head. "You must've been

upset when you saw Susan talking to one of your old boy-friends."

Lacy looked down and folded her hands in front of her and considered her answer for a few moments. She said flatly, "I was irritated, but I can't say I was surprised. Susan always attracted all the men, and she enjoyed the attention."

Detective Dagle leaned forward and raised his voice, "Come on, you must've been steaming. You got angry at her, didn't you?"

Lacy leaned back defensively and crossed her arms. "I did not kill Susan."

"Well, Susan is dead and Patricia is missing. What do you think happened?"

Lacy looked down. Her voice quivered. "I don't know. We got back to the houseboat and I opened a bottle of tequila. Patricia was taking meds, so she didn't drink. But Susan and I took a couple of shots and . . . that's the last thing I remember . . . until the cops woke me up . . . and I saw the blood."

Lacy started to tear up and sobbed while Detective Dagle stared at her intently.

Lacy took a deep breath. "That's all I remember. I don't know who took Patricia, and I don't know who killed Susan."

Detective Dagle made some notes for about a minute before he continued. "How long have you known Susan Kelly and Patricia Hendricks?"

Lacy smiled through her tears. "We met in our freshman year at Gainesville, and we became roommates in an apartment for our last three years until we graduated. We became close friends."

"So, you've been good friends since college?"

Lacy looked down for a few seconds before she said cautiously, "We've had our good times and bad times, but we've always stayed in touch. This last year was tough on all of us because of our divorces, so we've been talking and texting more. We're all on Facebook and we've seen pictures of what everybody is doing. We all love being around the water, so I suggested a girls' weekend, and Patricia suggested using the rental houseboat from her marina."

Detective Dagle looked down at his notes. "Let's talk about the bad times you had with Susan and Patricia. What do you mean by that?"

Lacy looked at the table and considered her answer for a few seconds. "Susan always had her choice of men because she was so pretty. I got upset a few . . . times when she . . . went out with men that I had dated."

Detective Dagle made a few notes on his pad before he looked up. "Let's talk about these men that . . . you both dated. Who was the first?"

Lacy leaned back in her chair and took a deep breath as her face tightened up. "This is very embarrassing for me to talk about . . . and now that Susan's dead . . ."

Detective Dagle knew he was on to something, but he didn't want to scare her too much as her voice trailed off. When he saw Lacy look down and put her face in her hands, he decided to switch his interview tactic and lowered his voice to a sympathetic tone. "Look Ms. Turner, we're going to investigate everything about you, Susan and Patricia, and what conflicts you had in the past. If you try and hide something, it'll make us suspicious of your story about not remembering anything. But if you tell us your side of the story, it'll help us believe you when you tell us you don't remember what happened on the houseboat."

Lacy looked at her feet for a few seconds and whispered. "I'm scared. I don't know if I should talk to you."

Detective Dagle sat back in his chair and debated his next move. He decided to continue in his sympathetic tone, "I understand this is a lot of questions at once, and I don't want to pressure you. I'm gonna go take a bathroom break for a few minutes, but while I'm gone, I want you to realize this is your only chance to tell us your side of the story. If you don't talk to us, all I know is I've got one victim missing and one victim dead. You've got to think about it from my perspective; I have to investigate this, and if you don't want to talk to me, it looks bad."

Detective Dagle stood up and walked slowly to the door. As he opened the door, he looked back at Lacy and said quietly, "I'll be back in a few minutes and you can let me know what you want to do."

Lacy nodded and Detective Dagle softly shut the door. During the next few minutes of the video, Lacy laid her head on the table and wept quietly. She finally sat up and wiped her tears and blew her nose with a Kleenex. She took a few deep breaths and stood up and stretched. After about five minutes, Detective Dagle opened the door and walked back into the room with two glasses of water and sat down.

He put one glass of water in front of Lacy. "I thought you might be thirsty."

Lacy nodded and took a long drink of the water and set the glass on the table. "Thank you," she whispered.

Detective Dagle smiled and said, "Take your time; we're not in a hurry."

After she took a few swallows of the water, Detective Dagle asked quietly, "Are you ready to tell me about you and Susan and the men you both dated?"

Lacy nodded and took a deep breath. "I had a steady boyfriend, Jason Winston, my last two years of college. I thought he was the one that I'd marry, have kids with, and live happily . . . ever after. Well, at the end of our last semester in our senior year, Susan finished her exams earlier than I did, so she'd packed up most of her stuff and drove back to her parent's house in Miami to unload. She was going to return for graduation the following week and get the rest of her junk. I was walking by her empty room and noticed her answering machine on the carpet, and it was blinking with a message, so I hit play."

Lacy bit her lip and started to cry. Detective Dagle just watched and waited for her to regain her composure.

After about a minute, Lacy wiped her tears away and continued gravely, "On the tape, I heard my boyfriend, Jason, apologizing about getting her pregnant and hoped she was recovering from the abortion."

Detective Dagle dropped his pen on the table, and the noise startled Lacy. Detective Dagle picked up his pen and said, "That must've made you crazy mad."

Lacy took a drink of water and cleared her throat. "I saw red and just started screaming. Patricia came in from the other room asking what was happening, and I played the message for her, and she yelled too."

"So, did you confront your boyfriend?"

"Oh yeah," Lacy said firmly while she nodded emphatically and gave a bitter smile. "He claimed it was a one night stand when they hooked up at a bar while I was working one night. And then, Susan claimed they hooked up over spring break in Ft. Lauderdale, again while I was working." Lacy shrugged and said quietly, "Who knows what the truth is."

Detective Dagle studied Lacy intently before he spoke a few seconds later. "I'm surprised you ever talked to her after that."

"It was a while," Lacy admitted.

"When did you next talk to her?"

Lacy thought for a second before a brief, mischievous smile crossed her face. "A few years later, when I was getting my doctorate in psychology, I started dating a guy I knew from undergrad, Greg Rushing. He had dated Susan for a while our junior year, but he'd dumped her because she cheated on him. So, we'd been dating for about six months and went to Key West for a vacation. While we were down there, we ran into Susan at a bar, and the look on her face was priceless. Later on that night, I saw her in the bar's bathroom, and she apologized to me about Jason, but I blew her off."

Detective Dagle scratched his left temple with his fingers before he spoke. "I bet it felt good to get a little revenge?"

Lacy shrugged. "I admit it was kinda fun to turn the tables on her that night, but the next morning, I was sad because I missed all the fun we used to have before I found out about her and Jason."

"When did you see her again?"

Lacy looked down and shook her head. "I don't like talking about our next meeting."

Detective Dagle didn't say anything, but kept staring at Lacy.

After about 15 seconds of silence, Lacy looked up and took a deep breath. "A few years later, I was at a seminar in

Miami Beach at the Fontainebleau Resort, and I hit the bar that night. I saw Susan's father, who was recently divorced, and he started buying us bottles of Dom Perignon. We got drunk and he invited me back to his place, and . . ."

Lacy looked down for a few second, took a deep breath, and then continued wistfully, "The next morning Susan shows up at her Dad's house and catches me there with her dad."

"Wow."

Lacy shook her head. "I'm not proud of myself."

Detective Dagle made some notes on his pad, and Lacy looked around the room nervously as she waited for the next question. At one point, she stared at the camera for a few seconds before she looked back at Detective Dagle.

"When did you next talk to Susan?"

"About a month later, I called her up and apologized. Slowly after that, we started talking about once a month, and Patricia always encouraged us to try and renew our friend-ship—she was always the peacemaker. A year or so later, all three of us went to Disney World for a long weekend, and we had a ball. After that Disney weekend, we became more forgiving of each other and started talking every week."

Detective Dagle leaned forward in his chair. "Did you and Susan ever date the same man again?"

Lacy put her head in her hands and slowly shook her head, but didn't speak for a few seconds. She finally looked up and said flatly, "I just got divorced last year from my husband of 12 years. The day we get the final divorce decree in the mail, he texted me and told me he had a fling with Susan while we were married. I confronted Susan about it, but she denied it ever happened. I don't know if he was just trying to piss me off, or if Susan was lying. Of course, it wasn't the first time my ex-husband had cheated on me, so who knows?"

Detective Dagle sat back in his chair and crossed his arms. "It's hard for me to believe that you and Susan could still be friends after all this. How's that possible after all of these things happened?"

"I don't know." Lacy shrugged and said softly, "We were both wrong, but we'd forgiven each other."

Detective Dagle looked at his notes and slowly shook his head for a few seconds. He decided it was time to change tactics, so he pointed at Lacy and said strongly, "Isn't it true, you killed Susan because you were mad at her for trying to steal another man from you?"

Lacy instinctively sat back in her chair and crossed her arms as she answered anxiously, "No, that's not true. I know all of this sounds bad, but I didn't do it."

"How do you know you didn't do it, if you can't remember? You were drunk and your true feelings came out and you killed her, didn't you?

Lacy shook her head furiously and started to tear up. "I

know I didn't kill her. I know I didn't."

Detective Dagle abruptly stood up and pointed at Lacy's chest. "How'd it feel when you sliced her neck open and her blood squirted all over your hands and blouse?"

Lacy instinctively looked down at the blood stains on her blouse, slowly shook her head, and started pleading in a raspy voice, "I know I didn't kill her."

Detective Dagle scratched his head and asked skeptically, "Is there anything else you want to say before I take you to the holding cell?"

Lacy busted out crying and put her head on the table.

Detective Dagle turned and faced the camera. "We're concluding this interview." He reached up towards the camera lens, touching a button out of view, and the screen went dark.

The courtroom was silent as the video ended and the assistant bailiff turned the lights back up to full strength. Judge Bronson looked at the jury. "We're going to take a 15 minute break and then resume the testimony of this witness."

*   *   *   *   *

"Mr. Powers, you may resume your questioning of the witness," Judge Bronson said.

Frank nodded at the judge and then looked toward the witness stand. "Detective Dagle, what actions did you take after this interview with the Defendant?"

Detective Dagle looked at the jury. "The first thing I did was track down all of the people the Defendant mentioned in her interview and questioned them. The second thing I did was subpoena all of the Defendant's Facebook posts and texts for the past year."

"Were you able to get all of the posts and texts the Defendant made, even if they'd been deleted?"

Detective Dagle looked smug as he sat up in his seat. "All texts and all posts are saved on the hard drives of the servers, even if they are deleted, for at least a year by all of the service providers and Facebook."

Frank looked over at the jury and noticed a few jurors smiling, and a few jurors looking uncomfortable. "Did you find any Facebook posts or texts from the Defendant that you would deem related to this case?"

Detective Dagle nodded and smiled. "Oh, yes. I have collected 15 that are very incriminating statements by the Defendant."

"Objection! Opinion evidence." Amanda announced emphatically as she stood up.

"Sustained." Judge Bronson said flatly.

Frank quickly rearranged his thoughts and continued. "Detective Dagle, have you collected 15 statements made by the Defendant on Facebook and texts that are related to a possible motive to murder the victim in this case?"

"Yes, I have." Detective Dagle gave Amanda a nasty glare.

Frank looked at Judge Bronson and said authoritatively, "Your Honor, I move to admit these statements."

"Objection, relevance," Amanda pleaded.

Judge Bronson looked over at Detective Dagle and asked, "How did you secure these statements?"

Detective Dagle turned toward Judge Bronson and cleared his throat. "Your Honor, I sent subpoenas to Facebook and the Defendant's phone company, and they replied with these documents that have been verified by their corporate legal division representatives as accurate."

Judge Bronson nodded and looked at Amanda. "Objection overruled. These documents are admitted, and they may be published on the courtroom's screen via the prosecutor's laptop."

Frank looked over at the assistant bailiff and he lowered the lights in the courtroom. "Detective Dagle, how did you arrange these 15 exhibits?"

"I have labeled them chronologically with the oldest being number one, up to the most recent being number 15. I then put a second line on the label, showing how long since the last post exhibited prior. When the Defendant is the speaker, I labeled it 'Lacy Turner.' When the speaker is the victim, I labeled it 'Susan Kelly.' And when it is the missing woman, I labeled it 'Patricia Hendricks.'"

Frank looked at Judge Bronson. "Your Honor, with the Court's permission, I have programmed my computer to display each exhibit for 45 seconds and then automatically go to the next exhibit."

Judge Bronson nodded. "You may publish the exhibits."

The assistant bailiff lowered the lights in the courtroom as Frank hit a button on his laptop. He looked over at the courtroom screen to watch the exhibits as the computer began the timed display.

State's Exhibit 1
Phone text – 5/1/14 @ 10:17 p.m.

Lacy Turner: U ruined my life by fucking Jason during college! He was gonna b the father of my children!!!

Susan Kelly: I'm sorry, I never meant to hurt u – I was drunk!!!

Lacy Turner: UR A WHORE!

State's Exhibit 2
Phone text – 5/3/14 @ 3:30 p.m.
Two days after Exhibit 1

Patricia Hendricks: Let's all go to Disney for Memorial Day Weekend!

Lacy Turner: I don't want to be around that whore in Disney, she'd probably try to fuck Goofy and Micky at the same time!

Patricia Hendricks: Come on, b nice – please?
Lacy Turner: Maybe we can go on space mountain & she'll fall off?!?!

Patricia Hendricks: DON'T TALK LIKE THAT!!!

Lacy Turner: why??? Can't I have a fantasy???

State's Exhibit 3
Facebook private message – 6/2/14 @ 8:19 p.m.
30 days after Exhibit 2

Lacy Turner: I saw your FB posts and pictures from your girls cruise over Memorial Day Weekend. Did you tell your husband you were going??? I counted you in pictures with at least 7 guys. Did you fuck them ALL?!?!

Susan Kelly: No – just the lucky ones!

Lacy Turner: U won't ever change, will u? U R STILL MARRIED!!!

Susan Kelly: We r separated and getting

divorced. why shouldn't I have some fun???

State's Exhibit 4
Facebook private message – 7/5/14 @ 9:21 p.m.
37 days after Exhibit 3

Susan Kelly: I just saw ur pics from the weekend at St. Pete Beach! Ur looking hot in that new bikini! How do you stay in such good shape???
Lacy Turner: I eat healthy and only fuck 1 man at a time. U should try it sometime!

Susan Kelly: why r u always so angry???

Lacy Turner: U MADE ME THIS WAY!!!

State's Exhibit 5
Facebook private message – 8/3/14 @ 5:30 p.m.
28 days after Exhibit 4

Patricia Hendricks: Let's all go to Disney for Labor Day weekend. I need to get out of town b/c my soon to b ex-husband always shows up when I'm out having fun. Can u say STALKER???
Lacy Turner: My soon to be ex always gives me shit too! Let's do Disney!!!

Patricia Hendricks: GREAT! I'll let Susan know!

Lacy Turner: Tell her it's a girls weekend – if she brings a strange man back to our room I'll kill her!

State's Exhibit 6
Text message – 9/2/14 @ 1:30 a.m.
29 days after Exhibit 5

Lacy Turner: I just put Patricia to bed after she threw up for 20 minutes!!! She started doing lemon drop shots after u left the bar with the guy she was talking to. Why do u ALWAYS hit on the men that WE want??? YOU WILL GET YOURS ONE DAY!!!!!!! I hope when u read this in the morning, after u leave his room, u will feel like shit! U made Patricia feel like shit and it reminded me of all the shit u did to me. UR a fucking WHORE!!!

State's Exhibit 7
Facebook private message – 10/31/14 @ 11:30 p.m.
59 days after Exhibit 6

Lacy Turner: I just looked at ALL of ur pics from the Halloween party. U took 34 selfies between 7:02 p.m. and 10:16 p.m. 34!!! It's a wonder that any man would talk to u be-

ing so obsessed with ur looks. But the last pic you posted an hour and 15 minutes ago was with a good looking hunk in front of his red Porsche! U r probably in his bed doing what u do BEST!!!

Susan Kelly: I just sent u a selfie of me in his bathroom. We just finished round one and I'm gonna make his toes curl with round two. It's too bad u r at home by urself, facebook stalking me because ur BORED! U should find a man to make ur toes curl instead of facebook stalking me!

Lacy Turner: I hate you! I hope he gives u AIDS & u die!

State's Exhibit 8
Facebook private message – 11/10/14 @ 11:33 p.m.
11 days after Exhibit 7

Lacy Turner: My ex-husband just sent me a text saying that he fucked you while we were married? REALLY!?!? My boyfriend and my husband???

Susan Kelly: I DID NOT FUCK YOUR HUSBAND! He hit on me once a few years ago @ the beach party and I told him NO!

Lacy Turner: Why should I believe you? YOU ALWAYS LIE! And fuck my men.

Susan Kelly   You fucked my FATHER!!!

Lacy Turner   I did fuck your father! When we were lying in bed later, he told me he was always disappointed in you!   And then I fucked him again!

State's Exhibit 9
Phone text – 11/29/14 @ 7:10 p.m.
19 days after Exhibit 8

Lacy Turner: I'm sitting across from u at this wedding reception and I can't believe u r all over my brother!!! He just got divorced from a slut and he doesn't need another slut in his life."

Susan Kelly: Look under the table and see where I have my hand on ur brother! He's so hot!!!

Lacy Turner: Please leave my brother alone!

State's Exhibit 10
Phone text – 11/29/14 @ 9:17 p.m.
Two hours, seven minutes after Exhibit 9

Lacy Turner: U think you're so hot in that tight little black dress dancing with my brother. The problem is that it's so tight it shows ur expanding muffin top and all the guys are pointing at it when ur back is turned!

Susan Kelly: They're looking at my ass, not my little muffin top!!!

Lacy Turner: How much weight have u gained since summer?

Susan Kelly: LOL! I just got back from a 2 week cruise with my new boyfriend and we ate and drank a lot, so yes, I have put on 6 pounds since u have seen me last. I think I'll work it off this weekend by fucking ur brother!

Lacy Turner: Leave my brother alone!!!

State's Exhibit 11
Facebook private message – 12/23/14 @ 8:30 p.m.
24 days after Exhibit 10

Lacy Turner: I'm looking at ur Christmas party pics and I can't believe u r still wearing that Santa's elf outfit u have had since college. U r too old to wear that outfit!

Susan Kelly: All the men like it, so I wear it and they always try to get me under the mistletoe! I think that's ur problem – no

*one has taken u under the mistletoe this
Christmas! You're turning into an old maid
and facebook stalking me because u aren't
having fun!*

*Lacy Turner: Go to hell! Unlike u, I'm
picky over who I spread my legs for!!!*

State's Exhibit 12
Phone text – 1/1/15 @ 2:17 p.m.
Eight days after Exhibit 11
*Lacy Turner: It's the New Year and I've
decided to try and get rid of all the negativ-
ity I've had about u these past few years.
U have made me so mad sometimes I've
wanted to kill u! But I'm turning over a new
leaf and I want us to be close again. I'd like
for Patricia and u to come and visit me in
Naples one weekend.*

*Susan Kelly: I'd like that!!! I'll call Patri-
cia and find out what weekend is good for
her.*

State's Exhibit 13
Phone text – 2/1/15 @ 6:03 p.m.
30 days after Exhibit 12

*Lacy Turner: That guy was hitting on Pa-
tricia, why did u have to butt in? Leave him
alone and let Patricia have some fun. There
are plenty of other men here at the bar*

Susan Kelly: OK, I was just talking to him

Lacy Turner: ur leaning over showing him your boobs! Why do u always try to take our men???

State's Exhibit 14
Phone text – 2/1/15 @ 10:17 p.m.
4 hours, 14 minutes after Exhibit 13

Lacy Turner: It was supposed to be a girls' weekend in Naples and now u have left us to go back to that guy's house and fuck him. I hope u r happy!!!

Susan Kelly: I'm sorry, but he's so CUTE!!! I'm riding in his black Maserati right now and it's so HOT!

Lacy Turner: All you care about is urself!!! I hope u crash & die!!!

State's Exhibit 15
Phone text – 5/15/15 @ 9:02 p.m.
104 days after Exhibit 14

Lacy Turner: He's my old boyfriend. STAY AWAY!!! U think u r so hot in that yellow sundress, but it's so tight it shows ur grow-ing muffin top. STAY AWAY OR ELSE!!!!!!!

There are plenty of other fishermen at Cabbage Key this weekend for u to fuck!

Susan Kelly: OK, OK. I was just talking to him

The slide show on Frank's laptop stopped and the screen went blank. Frank nodded to the assistant bailiff and he turned the lights in the courtroom back to full strength.

Frank was pleased that all of the jurors were staring at Lacy with angry faces. Frank looked at Judge Bronson. "No more questions, Your Honor."

Judge Bronson looked at the jurors. "We're going to break for the day; I'll see you back here at 9:00 a.m."

Chapter 9

Tuesday, August 18, 2015 at 5:50 p.m.

Ford's Garage Restaurant in Ft. Myers, Florida

Frank was enjoying a scotch at his table at Ford's Garage as he waited for Beth to join him for dinner. Ford's Garage was a restaurant in downtown Ft. Myers, named after one of Ft. Myers' most famous snowbirds, Henry Ford. Thomas Edison, Harvey Firestone, and Henry Ford were all neighbors in the 1920s along the river on McGregor Boulevard in downtown Ft. Myers. After their deaths, their families donated their homes to the City of Ft. Myers as a historical museum to honor their work. Ford's Garage has an old model T Ford parked on a display in the middle of the restaurant and other memorabilia to commemorate Ford's legacy.

It was a convenient place for dinner because it was only two blocks from the courthouse and one block from Beth's office. Their specialty was gourmet burgers made with Kobe Beef and any topping imaginable. Frank had been thinking about which juicy burger he wanted to order as soon as he entered and smelled the delicious aromas of sautéed onions and smoky Gouda cheese drifting throughout the restaurant. Frank saw Beth walk in the door and gave him a smile that made him forget the stress of the trial. As she walked toward him, he admired her fitted blue dress that showed off her womanly curves.

Frank stood up and gave Beth a polite kiss on the lips and whispered, "You're the best thing I've seen all day."

Beth beamed. "That's the nicest thing I've heard all day, so we're even." Beth sat down and leaned back in her chair. "How's the trial going?"

Frank shrugged. "It's hard to tell with this jury."

The waitress walked over. "What can I get you?"

Beth thought for a second. "I'd like a glass of Merlot and a Portobello Mushroom Burger, medium well."

The waitress nodded and looked at Frank. "What about you, sir?"

"I'll have the Blackened and Bleu Cheese Burger, loaded with everything," Frank said enthusiastically.

As the waitress walked away, Beth leaned forward and said quietly, "Tell me about the trial."

Frank took a deep breath and drained his scotch. "Everything was going as planned until the defense lawyer brought up that the Defendant and victim were friendly at the marina and Cabbage Key before the murder, so it had to be someone else. She brought up that we haven't proved who owned the knife that sliced the victim's throat. She also made a big deal out of the fact that we didn't compare the bloody footprints on the deck of the houseboat to the victim's or Defendant's feet size."

Beth raised her hands slowly and shook her head. "So, how did the bloody knife get her fingerprints on it if they were 'friendly' back at the houseboat?"

"Good question. But the defense lawyer is pretty skilled at trying to manipulate the jury." Frank shook his head and cracked his knuckles. "I don't know what the jury thinks."

The waitress brought Beth her wine and glasses of water for both her and Frank. After she walked away, Beth answered confidently, "Everybody knows a defense lawyer's job is to try and create doubt in the jury's mind. I wouldn't worry about it because all the evidence is in your favor. Once the jury gets all the evidence, they will realize Amanda is just throwing mud and hoping something sticks."

Frank took a deep breath. "I hope the jurors all think like you."

Beth grinned and gave a slight nod as she took a sip of her wine. Frank cracked his knuckles again and tried to relax.

"I need to go powder my nose," Beth said as she stood up.

She patted Frank on the shoulder, kissed his cheek and walked down the hall to the ladies' room with her purse. After she finished her necessities and washed her hands, she decided to put on some lipstick. As she concentrated on her lips in the mirror, she noticed the lines starting to form on each side of her lips and became flustered. She moved her glance up to her crow's feet at the edge of her eyes and thought they'd grown from the day before. Beth had thought about Botox or getting her eyes done, but it was hard to take a week off to let the bruising heal after the surgery. Many of Beth's female divorce clients got plastic surgery during the divorce to help their confidence as they re-entered the dating world, so she already knew the best doctors to call. One of her clients had told her a little nip and tuck was good for the soul, and the more Beth thought about it, the more she agreed. She decided to call tomorrow to make an appointment.

Beth had always wanted children when she was younger, but had cervical cancer when she was 20, so it wasn't an option. She enjoyed being around kids, and everyone called her the perfect aunt, but it still hurt her psyche that she couldn't have children. She used her nurturing instincts on her two cats, Bella and Gracie.

Beth had married her college sweetheart, Arthur "Artie" Zimba. Artie was a 5'10" baseball pitcher on scholarship at Mercer University and majored in English, along with Beth. He was a skinny left-hander and couldn't overpower hitters with a fastball, so he used change-ups and curve balls to strike out the other teams' batters. His freshman year, the game announcer dubbed him a "crafty left-hander," and the nickname stuck.

Beth and Artie started dating her junior year, right after she recovered from cervical cancer, and they married the summer after graduation. Before marriage, they had discussed the fact that Beth couldn't conceive, and Artie said he didn't care because he was in love with her and wanted to spend the rest of his life with her. Beth then started law school while Artie started teaching high school English and working on his master's degree. The summer before Beth's third year of law school, he came home one night and confessed to an affair with another teacher and that she was pregnant with his child. The next day, Beth decided she wanted to be a divorce lawyer, and she became her first client. She also started biting her nails again.

Beth didn't marry again until 14 years later when she was 39. She'd bought an old house in the historical area of Edison Park, near downtown Ft. Myers. The historical designation didn't allow houses to be torn down; they had to be renovated. Therefore, she had the house gutted down to the brick structure before she began renovations. She hired the sub-contractors to do all the required work and that was how she met her second husband, Alex Martinez.

Alex owned his own electrical company and was a very charming, second generation Cuban. His suave manners, good looks and high energy overwhelmed Beth's reservations about dating someone working on her house. Once they started dating, Beth felt like a love sick teenager - she thought of him all day and dreamed about him at night. After six months of dating, Beth proposed to Alex and he accepted.

During their sixth year of marriage, Alex had to do some rewiring at Beth's office and met Beth's young secretary. They started having an affair and hid it from Beth for three months. One morning at the breakfast table, Alex started crying and told Beth he was leaving her because her secretary was pregnant with his child. Beth started biting her nails again.

*   *   *   *   *

Frank was born and raised in Ft. Myers and lived there until he went away to college at the University of South Florida in Tampa. While he went to college in Tampa, he worked as a night security officer at the Port of Tampa. This job allowed him to study in between his rounds on the docks checking for thieves and drunks.

After he got his undergraduate degree in Economics, he went to law school at Florida State in Tallahassee. He worked as a part time law clerk for the State Attorney's Office in Tallahassee and that's where he developed his drive to be a career prosecutor. He watched more trials as a law student than most lawyers see in their career. By the time he graduated from law school, he was certain he wanted to return to his hometown and help keep it a safe place to live by sending the bad guys away to prison.

Frank's first murder trial happened after he'd been a prosecutor for four years. It was a classic case of a home burglary gone bad. The Defendant was a career thief with three prior burglary convictions and the elderly home owner came home during his lunch hour and surprised the Defendant. They had a struggle when the Defendant tried to escape and the home owner had a heart attack and died. After the Defendant was sent away to prison for life, Frank had deep sense of accomplishment that his hometown was a better place to live because he had performed well in court. At that point, Frank was certain he would be a prosecutor until retirement.

* * * * *

As Beth was walking back from the bathroom, she saw the waitress setting the tray of food down next to the table. As she sat down, the flavorful aroma of the hot burgers made her nose tingle with pleasure. The couple next to them eating chicken Caesar salads gazed jealousy at their burgers as the waitress served the meal.

Frank smiled and licked his chops. "My lunch of crackers and cheese wasn't very filling. I'm ready for a party in my mouth with this hunk of beef."

Beth winked. "Me too."

After they devoured their burgers and fries without talking, they sat back in their chairs and relaxed. Beth smiled and chuckled to herself.

Frank cocked his head and cracked a smile. "What's so funny?"

Beth said buoyantly, "I was at mediation this afternoon with a client that I've represented in three divorces over the years. She's an older southern belle from Shreveport, Louisiana with a great sense of humor, and she was telling jokes this afternoon during breaks in the mediation and cracking me up."

Frank said, "Tell me your favorite one."

Beth gave him a wacky smile and asked amusingly, "Why are blonde jokes are so short?"

Frank shook his head and smiled. "I have no idea."

"So men can remember them," Beth quipped.

Frank laughed and then held up his right pointer and asked, "Why don't junior leaguers believe in group sex?"

Beth shrugged and said jovially, "Don't know."

"All the thank you notes."

Beth nodded and smiled. "That's a good one. I've got to tell a few of my friends that one." Beth chuckled and held up her right pointer. "My client told me that among divorced women in their sixties at her country club, the saying is that older single men are just looking for women with purses or that can be nurses, and she didn't want either, so she was staying single. She said she was just going to date the young cabana boys when she needed some attention."

"Okay, that's an interesting perspective. I've got one for you," Frank said cheerfully as he held up his right pointer. "As I was leaving the courthouse for the lunch break, I was riding the elevator down with a group of male bailiffs, and they were talking about certain women at the courthouse that always date cops. I guess the cops call them 'holster sniffers!'"

Beth belly laughed and thought how comfortable her relationship was with Frank. She had never been able to talk intelligently and have such an intimate mental connection with any other man before. She leaned toward Frank and whispered, "I can't wait until we finish here and go home for dessert."

Frank's eyes widened and he looked over to the waitress. "Could we have our check, please?"

Chapter 10

Wednesday, August 19, 2015 at 9:01 a.m.

Courtroom 6B, Lee County Courthouse in Ft. Myers, Florida

"Good morning ladies and gentleman of the jury. I believe we're ready to get started this morning." Judge Bronson looked at Amanda. "The defense may cross-examine the witness."

Amanda walked to the podium with her notes and looked at Detective Dagle. "Isn't it true that you subpoenaed one year's worth of texts and Facebook posts for my client?"

"Yes, that's true." Detective Dagle nodded in agreement.

"Isn't it also true that there were 304 texts and private messages between my client and the victim during that year?"

Detective Dagle looked at his notes and nodded. "That's true."

"Isn't it true that the 15 texts and private messages you showed the jury between my client and the victim were less than five percent of the total communications between them in the past year?"

Detective Dagle shrugged and said flatly, "That sounds about right."

"Isn't it true that you chose to show the jury only a small portion of the communications between them because you were trying to mislead the jury?"

Detective Dagle shook his head and snickered. "No, that's not true. I only wanted to show them your client's motive for murdering the victim."

"Objection. Opinion evidence." Amanda pleaded.

Judge Bronson shook her head. "Overruled. He answered your question."

Frank looked at the jurors and saw two older men in the back row look at each other and smile.

Amanda took a deep breath and gathered her thoughts for a moment. "Isn't it true you didn't show the jurors the other ninety five percent of the messages because it didn't help your case?"

Detective Dagle considered his answer for a second. "The other messages were other private conversations not related to the motive to murder."

Amanda motioned with her right hand toward the ceiling and raised her voice. "Exactly! They were just normal communications between friends, weren't they?"

Detective Dagle shrugged and said sarcastically, "I guess so, but apparently they weren't really good friends because your client sliced her neck."

"Objection, opinion evidence," Amanda pleaded again.

"Sustained!" Judge Bronson said as she gave Detective Dagle the evil eye. "Please answer the question with no commentary, Detective."

Detective Dagle sat back in chair in a contrite manner and said evenly, "I suppose they were just normal texts between friends."

Amanda nodded, looked at her notes for a few seconds, and then back to Detective Dagle. "Isn't it true that the victim had burns on her nipples and her nostrils?"

Detective Dagle nodded and said flatly, "Yes."

"Isn't it true that you didn't find any cigarette lighters on board the houseboat?"

Detective Dagle sighed. "No, we didn't."

"Did you have a diver search the area around the houseboat for cigarette lighters or any other evidence?"

Detective Dagle leaned forward and spoke directly in the microphone. "Why would we when we caught your client red-handed?"

"Objection, non-responsive."

"Sustained." Judge Bronson leaned toward Detective Dagle and raised her voice. "Detective Dagle, just answer the question without your commentary. Do you understand?"

Detective Dagle nodded sheepishly and leaned back in

chair. "Yes, Your Honor."

Amanda looked smugly at Detective Dagle and asked in a saccharine voice, "Did any divers search the area around the houseboat?"

"No."

"In the interview with my client, didn't she tell you she couldn't remember what happened?"

"Yes."

Amanda held her hands out to her side. "Why didn't you take a blood sample from her to test for drugs or alcohol in her system?"

Detective Dagle shrugged. "We didn't think it was necessary."

"Isn't it true that the victim had bruising around her ankles and wrists?"

"Yes."

Amanda crossed her arms and raised her voice. "Isn't this evidence consistent with someone being bound to a chair while being tortured as they try to move and escape?"

Detective Dagle cleared his throat before he answered evenly. "Yes."

Amanda looked at the jury as she asked, "Would you consider someone being tied up nude to a chair and having their nipples and nostrils burned with a cigarette lighter torture?"

Detective Dagle nodded. "Most certainly, I'd consider

that torture."

Amanda turned back to Detective Dagle and pointed at him. "Isn't it true that torturing someone is a technique to get them to answer questions?"

Detective Dagle considered making a snide comment, but decided against it. "Yes."

Amanda looked down at her notes for a few seconds. "Isn't it true, that in the video of your interview of my client, you can see her hands on the table?"

"Yes, her hands are on the table during the interview."

"Aren't there red marks on her wrists?"

"Yes, but sometimes handcuffs leave marks."

"Aren't red marks on her wrists consistent with her being bound with rope?"

Detective Dagle shrugged. "I don't know about that."

Amanda pulled out two eight by ten inch pictures from under her notepad and looked at Judge Bronson. "Your Honor, I have two exhibits I'd like to show the witness. May I approach the witness stand?"

Judge Bronson nodded. "You may."

As Amanda walked to the witness stand with the pictures, she said, "For the record, I'm showing you the Defendant's exhibits 'A' and 'B'. Do you recognize them?"

Detective Dagle looked slowly at the pictures and then looked up. "I do. They're pictures of the Defendant's wrists and ankles taken at the jail. When we arrest someone, we take pictures of the suspect's entire body to document their condition when taken into custody. We do this for two reasons. One, we want to document what they looked like on the night of the arrest if the case goes to trial, and two, if an arrestee makes a claim we abused them during the arrest process, we have evidence to prove otherwise and protect ourselves.

Amanda looked at Judge Bronson. "Your Honor, I move to admit these pictures into evidence and publish them to the jury."

Judge Bronson nodded. "They're admitted. Please hand the pictures to the bailiff and he'll take them to the jury for viewing."

Amanda handed the pictures to the head bailiff and walked back to the podium. She waited for the jurors to pass the pictures between themselves and look at them. It took a couple of minutes, but once they'd all seen the two pictures, the head bailiff picked them up and put them on the counter in front of the clerk.

Amanda asked, "Detective Dagle, isn't it true that there are red marks around the Defendant's wrists and ankles?"

"Yes."

"Were handcuffs put around my client's ankles when she was brought to jail?"

Detective Dagle looked at his notes before answering slowly. "Your client didn't struggle when she was arrested, so her ankles were not bound."

Amanda held her hands out to her side. "How did red marks get around my client's ankles?"

Detective Dagle hesitated for a few moments and shrugged. "I don't know."

Amanda looked at the jury as she raised her voice for her final question. "If my client's wrists and ankles were tied together, how was she able to tie up the victim, torture her, and kill her?"

Frank stood up quickly. "Objection, assumes facts not in evidence."

"Objection sustained. The jury will disregard that question."

All of the jurors looked at the two pictures sitting on the counter in front of the clerk, and then at Lacy, and finally at Amanda. They all looked bewildered.

Amanda continued looking at the jury for a second before she looked at Judge Bronson and said confidently, "No further questions of this witness, Your Honor."

"You're dismissed, Detective Dagle." Judge Bronson said and then looked at Frank. "Please call your next witness."

Frank stood up. "The State calls Jason Winston."

The assistant bailiff walked to the witness room and opened the door. Jason Winston strutted to the front of the courtroom and was dutifully sworn in by the clerk. He was six feet, two inches tall and looked like a model for a jeans commercial, with long blond hair and possibly no more than four percent body fat filling out a tight red polo shirt and black jeans. He was wearing ostrich skinned cowboy boots and a heavy gold chain around his neck. He sat down in the witness stand, faced Frank and nodded confidently.

"Please give us your name and your address."

"My name is Jason Winston, and I live on Ocean Drive in Palm Beach, Florida."

Lacy snorted and crossed her arms in annoyance, which caused everyone in the courtroom to look at her. Amanda realized everyone was focused on her client, so she instinctively tried to minimalize the outburst by sympathetically patting Lacy on the back with her left hand. Judge Bronson gave a wary glance to Lacy, and she glanced down to avoid the unwanted attention.

"What do you do for a living?" Frank asked.

"I help my wife run the marina she owns down at the inlet," Jason said confidently and smiled at his wife in the audience area.

Amanda still had her hand on Lacy's back and could feel it stiffen up in annonyance, so she leaned over and whispered in Lacy's ear, "Keep it together. Everyone is watching you. If you have a bad reaction to him, the jury will think you have an uncontrollable temper and that you probably killed Susan."

Lacy looked down and nodded slightly.

Frank had glanced over at Amanda and Lacy and realized they were whispering. He decided to wait and ask his next question after they looked up, which would cause the jury to focus on Amanda whispering to her client. He hoped the jury would infer that the defense lawyer was coaching her guilty client on how to react to this damning testimony.

Amanda looked up when she realized there were no questions being asked, and saw that the jurors' attention was on her and Lacy. She silently stewed because she'd used the same technique when she was a prosecutor. She forced herself to remove her hand from Lacy's back and leaned back in her chair, crossing her arms and impatiently waited for Frank to continue.

Frank looked back at the witness. "How do you know the Defendant?"

Jason leaned back in his chair and looked at his wife, who stared intently at him, before he answered quietly. "Lacy and I used to date in college. It was a long time ago."

"Would you agree with me that you had a very serious relationship with her?"

Jason shrugged and said indifferently, "We dated about two years or so."

"Did you and she ever discuss getting married?"

Jason took a deep breath as he absorbed the laser stares from his wife and Lacy. "Lacy talked about it a few times, but I never said I wanted to marry her."

Lacy's face turned red, but she remembered Amanda's warning and didn't move. Jason again glanced at his wife, and she gave a forced smile, but her eyes were bulging with agitation.

"How did your relationship with Lacy end?"

Jason remembered the script he had written down a dozen times before trial that tried to minimalize his boorish behavior in college. He shifted in his chair and answered flatly, "Our last semester I knew I wanted to come back to my hometown of Palm Beach and begin my career. I also knew I didn't want to have anything serious with Lacy after we graduated, so I started spending more time with my friends and hoped she'd break it off without me having to hurt her feelings. But that didn't happen; she talked about us moving in together while she went to grad school. I knew I didn't want that, so I started dating a different girl and spending even less time with her—I hoped she'd get the hint, but she didn't."

"Was that girl the victim, Susan Kelly?"

Jason nodded. "It was."

"Had you told Lacy that you were dating her roommate and friend, Susan?"

Jason shook his head and answered in a shaky voice. "No, I just sort of hoped she'd get mad at me because I wasn't spending a lot of time with her and break up with me. I was hoping she'd understand that I was pulling away from her, and she'd assume I was dating someone else, and not ask questions. I didn't want to hurt her feelings by being blunt with her and tell her I was dating someone else."

"At some point in time after you started dating Susan, did she tell you she was pregnant?"

Jason looked down and said weakly. "She did."

"What happened after that?"

Jason considered his answer for a few moments before he said awkwardly, "She said she wanted an abortion and I agreed because I wasn't ready to start a family." Jason looked down and cleared his throat. "I took her to the clinic and paid for it. Afterward, I took her home, and she told me she wanted to be alone for a few days."

Frank hesitated and let the jury digest this embarrassing disclosure. He looked over at Lacy's flushed face and hoped the jury would follow his gaze. After a few seconds, he looked at the jury and saw they were all looking at Lacy intently. Amanda was giving Frank a laser stare, but he couldn't have cared less.

Frank asked sympathetically, "When did you next talk to Susan?"

Jason looked up and considered his answer for a moment. "I called her apartment number and got her answering machine. I left a message and asked how was she doing."

"A few hours later, did you receive a call from your

longtime girlfriend, Lacy?"

"Oh yeah." Jason looked down and said remorsefully, "She'd listened to the message on the answering machine and she went berserk." He looked up at Lacy momentarily and then back at Frank, before he continued in a serious tone. "She said she was going to kill me and then kill Susan."

Frank slowly looked over at Lacy and then back to Jason. "Did you ever talk to Susan Kelly after this?"

Jason shook his head slowly. "No, we never talked again."

"No further questions, Your Honor."

Judge Bronson looked at Amanda. "Cross-examination, counselor?"

Amanda stood up and walked to the podium without any notes. Once she had gripped the podium with her left hand, she pointed at Jason with her right pointer as she asked, "Isn't it true, that you had sex with Lacy at your apartment the night before you left that message on Susan's answering machine?"

Jason swallowed hard and glanced at his wife before he looked at his feet and contemplated his answer. "Lacy had the closing shift at Hooter's that night and she stopped by my apartment after work. I'd been drinking with my friends and I was drunk. I should've said no, but I didn't."

Amanda asked sternly, "So, your answer is yes, you had sex with Lacy the night before you left that message on

Susan's phone?"

Jason nodded and said meekly, "Yes."

Amanda held her hands out to her side. "So, while your new girlfriend was recovering from an abortion, you had sex with your old girlfriend?"

Jason's face turned beet red and the veins in his neck became visible. After a few awkward seconds, he simply answered, "Yes."

Lacy's right fingers were bouncing up and down on the defense table as she silently ground her teeth, and glared angrily at Jason. Frank glanced at the jurors and they were all looking at Jason with disdain.

Amanda shook her head in disgust and said scornfully, "No further questions of this witness, Your Honor."

Judge Bronson looked sideways at Jason and said curtly. "You're dismissed, sir. Now, please leave my courtroom." As everyone in the courtroom watched Jason leave, Judge Bronson looked at the jury. "We're going to take an hour for lunch. I'll see you back at 1:00 p.m."

Chapter 11

Wednesday, August 19, 2015 at 11:59 a.m.

Courtroom 6B, Lee County Courthouse in Ft. Myers, Florida

Everyone in the courtroom was standing as Judge Bronson walked off the bench toward her private exit. After the door closed, Amanda looked at Lacy and asked sympathetically, "How are you doing?"

Lacy shifted her stance and smiled weakly as she said quietly, "The good news is you had a great morning on cross-examination of the witnesses. I think the jury was paying attention to your points." Lacy then took a deep breath, looked down and blushed. "The bad news is I just relived one of the worst times of my life in a very public arena."

Amanda reached over and squeezed her hand. "I promise you, I'll get us through this mess."

Lacy raised her eyebrows wearily and nodded slowly. "I hope so." Lacy straightened out her arms to her side, stretched, and looked hopefully at Amanda. "I need some fresh air outside the courthouse. Do you want to get some lunch?"

Amanda shook her head quickly. "No, thanks. I'm going to the law library on the first floor to get ready for the afternoon witnesses. I've got a five hour energy drink and a granola bar in my briefcase for a quick lunch, while I prep. I'll see you back here ten minutes before we start back. Remember, if you see any of the jurors walking outside over lunch, smile, turn, and walk away from them. The Judge's instructions to the jurors are that they can't talk to any of the lawyers or participants during the trial, but a smile goes a long way."

Lacy gave a forced fake smile. "Got it. See you in a little while."

Amanda gave her own bogus smile and a thumbs-up sign. "Sounds good."

Amanda watched Lacy walk out of the courtroom while she gathered her notes and put them in her briefcase. This was the first time that Amanda had ever represented a friend in a criminal trial, and it definitely added stress to the trial. One part of a lawyer's job at trial is to remain emotionally detached so she could make strategic decisions without worrying about a client's feelings. It was definitely harder to do this when she had a personal relationship with a client. Amanda silently promised herself that she'd never represent a friend at a trial again. Especially a murder trial.

*   *   *   *   *

Amanda Blayne's father was an Air Force pilot, and he was stationed at Patrick Air Force base in Cocoa Beach, Florida while she was growing up. Her mother was a third grade teacher at a public school in the poor section of Cocoa Beach. Amanda was an only child and attended the same elementary school that her mother taught, so she was exposed to many different types of background by her classmates. It gave her an education on different cultures and made her appreciate the lifestyle she enjoyed with her parents.

Amanda was always very athletic while growing up, but she didn't like team sports. She didn't like to depend on anyone else to define her athletic success. She excelled at track, swimming and tennis in middle school. However, once she reached high school, she decided that track and cross country were the only sports that interested her. She excelled at these sports and set state high school records in the mile, two mile and cross country course in her junior year. She broke these records in her senior year, and they remained unbroken by anyone in the state since.

Amanda received a track scholarship to the University of Florida and got a double major in English and Psychology. During her sophomore year, Amanda had a few psychology classes with Lacy, and that was where there friendship started. After graduation, Lacy stayed in Gainesville to get her masters in psychology and Amanda went to law school at the University of Miami. They stayed in touch and usually met up at homecoming or other events at the University of Florida.

After law school, Amanda became a state court prosecutor in Miami for five years and then became a federal prosecutor for seven years. Her conviction rate during her 12 years as a prosecutor was 94%, and she was very proud of that fact. After her public embarrassment over her affair with a married fellow prosecutor, she decided to leave the U.S. Attorney's Office and hang her own shingle as a criminal defense lawyer in downtown Miami.

Amanda's first big trial as a defense lawyer was defending a man arrested for armed robbery at the Fontainebleau Hotel on Miami Beach. A rich Canadian tourist was robbed in the parking lot, and the police arrested the Defendant two days later based on a photo shown to the victim. During the trial, Amanda exposed the flawed procedures the police used when showing the victim an overly suggestive photo line-up. She also had three alibi witnesses for the Defendant, and the jury returned a not guilty verdict after 20 minutes of deliberation.

The media loved a former prosecutor exposing the lack of training of the police officers and sloppy police procedures. She gave multiple interviews to every television station and newspaper in the area after the trial. Her sharp intellect and athletic physique allowed her to become a media darling overnight. This flood of publicity caused her phones to ring non-stop for months, and she promptly doubled her retainer fee to cash in on this big win.

Her next big trial was six months later when she defended a Miami Dolphins football player that was accused of date-rape. It was a classic he said/she said case of alleged rape versus consensual sex. Amanda spent a full day cross-examining the alleged victim and pointed out many inconsistencies in her testimony. After two days of deliberation, the jury returned a not guilty verdict. After this huge win, she doubled her retainer fee again, but her client list kept expanding.

When Amanda got the call from Lacy about the murder charge she was facing in Ft. Myers, she quickly agreed to represent her old friend, even though she normally didn't take cases on the west coast of Florida. Amanda couldn't imagine that her friend from college was capable of such a brutal slaying, so she was determined to help her. However, after she got the evidence from the prosecutor during the discovery process, she realized that she was facing an uphill battle at trial with Lacy's fingerprints on the murder weapon and no one else left on the houseboat. She knew it was going to take every ounce of talent she had, a little luck, and Lacy performing well on the witness stand to win the case.

Chapter 12

Wednesday, August 19, 2015 at 1:10 p.m.

Courtroom 6B, Lee County Courthouse in Ft. Myers, Florida

Frank looked at the assistant bailiff. "The State calls Greg Rushing."

The assistant bailiff walked to the witness room, opened the door, and motioned to the witness. Greg Rushing walked to the front of the courtroom and was sworn in by the clerk. He was 5'11" and looked like a fishing guide with khaki pants and an orange Columbia fishing shirt with the top two buttons undone. He obviously worked outside because he had a tan face with white circles around his eyes, the tell-tale sign of wearing sunglasses on a daily basis. He sat down in the witness stand, faced Frank and smiled.

"Please give us your name and address."

"My name is Greg Rushing. I live at the Oasis condos in downtown Ft. Myers."

"What do you do for a living?"

"I'm a contractor, and I specialize in custom homes."

Lacy's face was back to its normal shade, but she still

looked uncomfortable as she sat up in her chair and started tapping her right pointer on the table.

Frank pointed toward Lacy. "How did you first meet the Defendant?"

Greg leaned back in his chair and considered his answer for a second. "We met at a fraternity party when she was in undergrad at the University of Florida. I'd been dating Susan for about a month, and she brought Lacy to one of our parties."

"When you say Susan, do you mean Susan Kelly, the victim in this case?"

Greg nodded. "I do."

"How long did you date Susan Kelly?"

"Not long." Greg shrugged. "Maybe two months."

"After you and Susan broke up, did you and Lacy stay friends?"

Greg cleared his throat before he answered. "Lacy worked at Hooter's, and I probably went there once a week with friends, so we stayed in touch."

Frank held his hands out to his side. "At some point, did you and Lacy start dating?"

Greg nodded. "We did. I was in my senior year of college and Lacy was in her first year of grad school, getting her doctorate in psychology."

"How long did you date?"

Greg shrugged. "I guess we dated for about a year or so.

I was partying pretty hard and I don't think Lacy approved, so we kinda drifted apart."

Frank nodded and looked at his notes for a moment. "Did you and Lacy ever go to Key West while you were dating?"

Greg smiled as a pleasant memory crossed his mind. "We did. We went to Fantasy Fest one year."

Frank cocked his head to the left. "While you both were in Key West, did you see Susan at one of the bars there?"

"We did." Greg leaned forward and smiled. "We ran into her at Sloppy Joes' Bar, and she gave us a bad stink eye."

"What do you mean?"

"When we walked in, Susan was sitting at the bar with a few of her friends doing shots. She saw us and gave us an angry look. Lacy grabbed my hand, and we just walked to the other side of the bar and ordered a drink."

"What happened next?"

Greg shook his head and snickered. "It was pretty intense. After two shots, Lacy pulled me close and gave me a wet kiss right in the middle of the bar with everybody watching and grabbed my ass with both hands. So, I grabbed her ass, lifted her up, and twirled her around. We got a bunch of cheers!"

Frank looked over at Lacy, who was looking at her feet and tapping her left fingers on the table. Frank looked back at Greg and pointed his right hand at him. "Did Lacy ever explain why she kissed you like that in the middle of the bar?"

"Yes, she did." Greg cleared his throat and took a deep breath before he continued in a subdued voice. "We got a table and had a few drinks, and she told me about her ex-boyfriend and Susan. I kinda sympathized with her because I broke up with Susan after she cheated on me."

"Did you ever see Susan and Lacy together in the bar?"

Greg shifted in his chair. "Sort of. Lacy went to the bathroom a while later, and I saw Susan follow her in there. Lacy told me later Susan tried to apologize in the bathroom, but she blew her off."

Frank looked at Judge Bronson. "No further questions, Your Honor."

Judge Bronson looked at Amanda. "Do you have any questions for cross-examination?"

Amanda stood up. "Just a few, Your Honor."

After Amanda walked casually to the podium and looked at Greg, she asked in a pleasant tone, "How long did you and Lacy stay in Key West after that night you saw Susan?"

Greg scratched his head for a second. "That happened the first night we got there, and we were there for a long weekend, so we stayed another two nights."

"Did Lacy ever mention Susan after that night at Sloppy Joe's Bar?"

Greg shook his head. "Not that I remember."

"After you returned from Key West, did Lacy ever talk about Susan to you again?"

Greg shook his head. "No."

"No further questions, Your Honor."

Judge Bronson looked at Greg and smiled. "You're dismissed, sir."

After Greg walked through the swinging gate on the divider separating the audience area from the counsel tables and bench, Judge Bronson looked at Frank. "Please call your next witness."

Frank looked at the assistant bailiff. "The State calls Randy Moore."

The assistant bailiff walked to the witness room and opened the door, motioning for the witness. Randy Moore walked to the front of the courtroom and was sworn in by the clerk. He was a stocky, five foot, 10 inch tall man with sparkling blue Irish eyes and light brown hair with a fresh crew cut. He wore a plaid green button down shirt, pressed khakis with freshly shined Cordovan loafers. He sat down in the witness stand and smiled at the jury.

"Please give us your name and address."

"My name is Dr. Randy Moore, and I live in a condo on Gulfshore Boulevard in Naples."

"What do you do for a living, Dr. Moore?"

"I have a psychology practice in Naples."

Frank pointed toward the defense table. "How do you know the Defendant, Lacy Turner?"

Dr. Moore turned and looked at Lacy stoically for a few seconds. "We used to be business partners in a psychology practice in Naples, but we split up about three years ago, and I practice by myself at this point."

"How long were you and the Defendant, Lacy Turner, business partners?"

Dr. Moore considered his answer for a few seconds. "We were together just one month shy of four years."

"Can you tell the jury what caused you and Lacy to end your business partnership?"

Dr. Moore nodded and cleared this throat. "I can. I had just gotten divorced a few months before, and I was at a Christmas Eve party at a mutual friend's house enjoy-ing myself. Lacy came to the party with Susan Kelly, and I started talking to her and Lacy wasn't happy. Susan and I exchanged numbers, and we eventually started dating. Lacy was very upset about it, so she gave me an ultimatum—ei-ther I stopped dating Susan or she was going to end our business partnership. So, I told her to have her lawyer draw up the business dissolution papers because I was very happy dating Susan . . . at least . . . I was at the time."

Frank crossed his arms. "Did Lacy tell you about the tangled friendship history between her and Susan?"

Dr. Moore considered his answer for a moment. "She

did, and I talked to Susan about it, also. Susan told me it was water under the bridge as far as she was concerned. She said when she was young and stupid, she had some indiscretions, but she'd moved on and she hoped Lacy had too."

Frank pointed to the defense table. "Did it appear to you that Lacy had moved on?"

Dr. Moore stroked his chin slowly and took a deep breath. "That's a hard question for me to answer because I was so close to the situation. Lacy and Susan had obviously become friends again because Lacy invited her to the Christmas party, but as soon as Susan and I started dating, something snapped. My intuition and training told me that Lacy was scared to have Susan close to any men in her life because of their history."

Frank was satisfied with the answer and looked at Judge Bronson. "No further questions, Your Honor."

Judge Bronson looked at Amanda. "Any questions for cross-examination?"

"Yes, Your Honor," Amanda said as she approached the podium. After she had arranged her notes, she looked up at Dr. Moore. "How long did you and Susan Kelly date?"

Dr. Moore cleared his throat and sat back in his chair. "We dated about seven months."

"Where was Susan Kelly living and working while you were dating her?"

"She was living in an apartment in Miami and working a

147

few miles from there at a gym as an aerobics instructor and personal trainer."

Amanda held her hands out to her side in a questioning manner. "Did she drive over for the weekends to see you?"

Dr. Moore nodded. "Yes, after she finished her aerobics class on Saturday mornings, she'd drive over and stay until Monday nights, and then drive back."

Amanda looked at her notes before she continued. "Did Susan ever complain about the driving to and from Naples?"

Dr. Moore crossed his arms in irritation. "Not exactly."

Amanda asked in a sweet voice, "Could you explain that further, please?"

Dr. Moore sighed. "She didn't mind the drive, but her car had over 200,000 miles on it, and she was worried about it breaking down. She was always asking me to get her a new car."

Amanda smiled and asked innocently, "So, did you buy her a new car?"

Dr. Moore looked sheepish. "I did."

Amanda raised her eyebrows. "What kind of car did you buy her?"

Dr. Moore looked down and took a deep breath before he answered. "I bought her a new black 650i BMW convertible."

There were a few people in the audience that audibly groaned. Frank looked at the jury and two female jurors were slowly shaking their heads. One male juror looked angry.

Amanda waited for the sounds to die down before she continued. "Isn't it true, that Susan broke up with you two weeks after you purchased this car for her?"

Dr. Moore's face flushed red and he glared at Amanda. "Yes."

Amanda looked at Judge Bronson. "No further questions, Your Honor."

Judge Bronson looked at the jury. "We're going to have a 15 minute afternoon break."

*   *   *   *   *

Frank looked at the assistant bailiff. "The State calls Adam Luce."

Lacy abruptly leaned back in her chair and crossed her arms in frustration. All of the jurors and Judge Bronson instinctively looked at Lacy. Amanda reached over and patted her back sympathetically for a moment, while giving her a warning glance.

The assistant bailiff walked to the witness room, opened the door, and called his name. Adam Luce walked to the front of the courtroom and was sworn in by the clerk. He was a tall, thin man with green eyes and gray hair that was receding in the front but hanging to his shoulders in the back.

149

He wore a rumpled white button down shirt and olive cotton pants with white Nike running shoes. He sat down in the witness stand, nodded at Judge Bronson, and smiled. Judge Bronson smiled back and seemed to enjoy having Adam so close to her.

Frank looked at the witness and said, "Please give us your name and address."

"My name is Adam Luce, and I live at the Quail Run apartments in North Naples."

"What do you do for a living, sir?"

"I've been a fireman for the Naples Fire Department for 18 years," Adam said proudly.

Frank pointed to Lacy. "How do you know the Defendant, Lacy Turner?"

Adam sat up in his chair, looked briefly at Lacy, and back toward Frank. "She was my wife for 12 years, but we've been divorced now for about a year. Her married name was Lacy Turner Luce, but she always said it was pronounced 'Lacy, turn her loose!'"

Three of the jurors snickered at Adam's joke, but Judge Bronson gave them a sideways glare and they were quickly stone-faced again. Lacy gave her ex-husband a laser stare that could have cut through steel.

Frank let the courtroom get quiet again before he asked, "Did you ever have any children together?"

Adam shook his head. "Naw, I wanted children, but

Lacy never found time for it."

Lacy slammed her hands on the table in front of her and Amanda quickly turned and put her hand on Lacy's back and whispered in her ear.

Judge Bronson looked directly at Lacy and banged her gavel. She said sternly, "There will be order in my court-room! No more outbursts, or I'll have the bailiff secure you so it'll be impossible for you to move."

Amanda stood up. "Your Honor, we apologize. There will be no more showing of emotion by the Defendant, but I'd ask that you instruct the witness to not make any com-ments that are meant to inflame the Defendant."

Judge Bronson turned nodded strongly at Adam. "The Defense's point is well taken. Mr. Luce, I'm instructing you not to answer a question with a hidden dig at your ex-wife. Do I make myself clear?"

Adam slumped back in his chair and muttered, "Yes, Your Honor."

Frank waited a few seconds before he continued. "Mr. Luce, do you recall the day you got the final judgment from the divorce in the mail?"

Adam nodded. "I do. I'd just gotten off a 24 hour shift at the station and stopped by a dive bar for a few beers before I went home. After I got home, I opened the mail and saw the final judgment."

"What did you do after that?"

Adam leaned back in his chair and crossed his arms. "The first thing I did was have another beer to celebrate. The second thing, I wished I hadn't done it, but I sent Lacy a text."

"What did the text say?"

Adam scratched his chin and looked down for a second before he responded. "It said, 'I just got the divorce papers and I'm the happiest I've been in 12 years. Now that we're divorced, I want you to know that Susan and I had an affair two years ago.'"

Frank looked over at Lacy who was red-faced and then back at Adam. "How did she respond?"

"Not well." Adam cleared his throat and continued, "She called me up and cussed me out, but I yelled back at her, too. I finally hung up, and she kept calling back. I finally just turned my phone off."

Frank held his hands up and raised his voice. "Did you and Susan have an affair?"

Adam took a deep breath and nodded slowly. "Yes. We were all away on a beach weekend with a bunch of people, and we snuck into one of the rooms while everybody else was at the beach. We saw each other a few times after that when I went to Miami on my days off."

Lacy's face was crimson, and she looked away from Adam. Amanda leaned over and patted her gently on the back.

Frank looked at Judge Bronson. "No further questions, Your Honor."

Judge Bronson looked at Amanda. "Any cross-examination?"

Amanda nodded and glared at Adam as she walked to the podium. After she got to the podium, she gripped it with her left hand and pointed at Adam. "Isn't it true that in your divorce settlement papers your ex-wife got half of your pension for the time you were married?"

Adam nodded and said curtly. "Yep, she sure did."

"Were you happy about this?"

Adam glared at Lacy for a moment before he said sarcastically, "What do you think, smarty pants?"

Judge Bronson snapped her head toward Adam. "Mr. Luce! You will refrain from asking questions to the lawyer and making snide remarks. That's the third time you have done this, and I'm done warning you. The next time is going to cost you 10 days in jail. Do I make myself clear?"

Adam's face turned white and he nodded. "Yes, Your Honor."

Amanda decided to end on this high note. "No further questions of this witness, Your Honor."

Judge Bronson looked at Adam, sat back in her chair and folded her arms as she said sharply, "You're dismissed."

Adam walked off the witness stand and looked smugly at Lacy. All of the jurors saw this parting shot and glared at

Adam as he walked out of the courtroom. Judge Bronson started to reprimand Adam, but she thought it was better just to get him out of her courtroom so the trial wasn't disrupted any more than it already was by his behavior.

She turned to Frank and said politely, "Please call your next witness."

Frank looked at the assistant bailiff. "The State calls Peter Turner."

The assistant bailiff walked to the witness room, opened the door, and called his name. Peter Turner walked to the front of the courtroom and was sworn in by the clerk. He was a tall, trim man with blue eyes and long, sandy hair. He wore a wrinkled Kelly green polo shirt and blue jeans with old weathered Topsiders. He sat down in the witness stand and looked uncomfortably toward Lacy and then at Frank.

Frank asked, "Can you please give us your name and where you live?"

Peter leaned awkwardly toward the microphone and spoke hesitantly. "My name is Peter Turner, and I live in Key West, Florida."

"What do you do for a living, Mr. Turner?"

Peter smiled slightly. "I'm a bartender."

Frank pointed toward Lacy. "How do you know Lacy Turner?"

Peter looked uneasily toward Lacy, and then back at Frank, before he answered blandly, "She's my sister."

There were a few murmurs in the courtroom, but Judge Bronson quieted everyone with an abrupt stare. Lacy looked at her brother nastily and crossed her arms. A few of the jurors looked at each other, eyebrows raised.

After everyone quieted down, Frank asked, "Did you know the victim in this case, Susan Kelly?"

Peter cleared his throat. "Yes. We met at a wedding and dated for a few months after that."

Frank pointed toward Lacy. "Did your sister approve of you dating Susan?"

Peter shook his head and looked down for a few seconds before he answered. "No. Lacy told me that Susan was trouble, and I shouldn't go out with her."

"Did you and Lacy have an argument about you dating Susan?"

"Oh, yes. Our argument was very ugly," Peter lamented. "We've only spoken a few times since then."

Frank raised his hands, palms up, and asked, "During this argument, did your sister ever make a threat towards Susan?"

Peter nodded and said quietly, "She said that she'd kill her if she hurt me."

Frank crossed his arms, looked at Lacy for a moment, and then back to Peter. "After you and Susan dated a few months, didn't she break up with you?"

Peter answered dismally, "Yes."

155

Frank raised his voice. "Were you hurt when she broke up with you?"

Peter shifted in his chair and stared at Frank for a few seconds before said evenly, "Yes."

Frank looked over at Lacy, shook his head slightly, and then looked at Judge Bronson. "No further questions, Your Honor."

Judge Bronson looked toward Amanda. "Do you have any questions for cross-examination?"

"I do," Amanda said as she walked to the podium. Once at the podium, Amanda looked at Peter and asked, "Your sister was very concerned when you started dating Susan, correct?"

Peter nodded. "Yes."

Amanda held up her right pointer. "Isn't it true, your sister told you about all of the men that Susan had broken up with over the years and hurt their feelings?"

"She did."

"Did a detective from the Lee County Sheriff's Office interview you about your relationship with Susan Kelly?"

Peter crossed his arms. "Yes. He told me that there were some texts between Susan and Lacy about the first time we met at a friend's wedding."

"Is that when you told the detective about the conversation your concerned sister had about you dating Susan Kelly?"

"Yes. He asked me if I ever heard Lacy threaten Susan, and that's when I told him about the threat."

Amanda held out her hands and slowly closed them before she asked incredulously, "Wasn't your sister just being protective of you when she said that to you?"

Peter shrugged and answered uncomfortably, "That's what I used to think. At least, until Susan was killed, that is. As I look back at it now, I sometimes wonder if I shouldn't have told Susan what Lacy told me. If she knew what Lacy had said, maybe she never would have gotten on the house-boat with her."

Amanda shook her head in disgust, looked at the jury hopefully for a moment, and then to Judge Bronson before she said flippantly, "No further questions of this witness, Your Honor."

Judge Bronson looked at Frank. "Please call you next witness."

Frank stood up, cleared his throat, and said authorita-tively, "There are no more witnesses, Your Honor. The State rests."

Judge Bronson smiled widely and looked at the jurors. "Ladies and gentleman of the jury, the State has rested. We're going to break for the day and the Defense will start its case tomorrow morning at 9:00 a.m. You're dismissed for the day."

Judge Bronson waited until the jury had walked out of

the courtroom before she left the bench. The head bailiff said good night as she opened a private door to the left of her bench and walked down a short hallway to the judges' private elevator to go back to her chambers on the ninth floor. As she waited for the elevator, she thought about the State's case against Lacy Turner and all of the witnesses that had testified. The defense lawyer had done a good job of trying to create reasonable doubt, but at the end of the day, Lacy's fingerprints were proven to be on the murder weapon and Lacy was found where the murder occurred. Judge Bronson was convinced it was going to be a guilty verdict unless Lacy did an exceptionally fantastic job on the witness stand.

Chapter 13

Wednesday, August 19, 2015 at 6:52 p.m.

The Veranda Restaurant in Ft. Myers, Florida

The history behind the Veranda restaurant had always intrigued Frank. Formed in 1971, an old Southern plantation home had been lifted from its original supports and moved 200 feet next door to an adjoining old plantation home, where a modern kitchen was built between them. It stood a wooden building with an old Southern décor in the middle of the downtown cement jungle.

Frank and Beth entered together, walking up wide brick steps to the large wooden doors, painted white, with artistic wrought iron grills and stained glass at eye level. The doors opened to a large parlor area with a high ceiling and a piano bar in the middle of the room, and they immediately smelled the welcoming aroma of freshly seared steak with sautéed onions. As they entered, Frank noted the waiting area and hostess' podium to the left with thick wrought iron windows looking out over the parking lot. To the right stood an L-shaped bar that ends at a swinging door going back to the kitchen. Past the L-shaped bar, a floor-to-ceiling wine rack was mounted on the wall, and behind the piano bar was a large fireplace that separated the sections of the restaurant.

A hallway to the dining room veered to the right of the fireplace, and the windowed terrace to the left looked out over a lush garden dining area outside, bordered by oak trees and bamboo clusters. It was a balmy night with a steady breeze, so Frank and Beth asked to be seated outside in the courtyard, by the koi pond. The Veranda was one block from the courthouse, so it became a favorite spot for law-yers, judges, politicians, and downtown business people. A common joke among local lawyers, including Frank, was that more cases have been settled at the Veranda than in the courthouse.

*   *   *   *   *

After the hostess seated them, Frank was quiet and looked across the shallow pond at the bamboo shoots that went 30 feet in the air. Beth knew Frank was exhausted, so she sat quietly and watched the koi swimming, giving him time for his thoughts.

The waitress walked up to the table. "Good evening. Can I bring you drinks?"

Frank nodded. "Scotch on the rocks."

Beth said, "A vodka and tonic, please."

After the waitress walked away, Beth asked, "How did the jury react to all of the fireworks today?"

Frank slowly shook his head. "There was so much dirty laundry in today's testimony, I feel like I need to go home and take a hot shower to get it off me."

Beth reached forward and placed her right hand supportively on top of his hand. "But you had to bring it all out to show Lacy's motive for murder, right?"

Frank nodded and sighed. "It wasn't pretty, but neither was the murder."

Beth noticed that all of the koi had gathered on the side of the pond closest to them, obviously fed by prior customers and looking for a handout. Frank moved his head from side to side, cracking his neck, as he tried to decompress from the stressful trial. His witnesses had finished, but their testimony had definitely not been pretty, and Amanda has scored a few points for the defense with her effective cross-examination.

"What do you think will happen tomorrow?" Beth asked.

Frank shrugged and said complacently, "In opening statement, Amanda said Lacy was going to testify, so my guess is that she'll be on the stand most of the day trying to explain all of the texts and private messages on Facebook. Of the 15 texts and private messages we presented, she talked about Susan dying in four of them."

Beth leaned forward and asked incredulously, "Really? What about the others?"

"Lacy calls her a slut and a whore and threatens her in the rest," Frank shook his head slowly in disgust. "If that's how she talks to friends, I'd hate to see how she talks to enemies."

Beth smiled slightly and gave Frank a sympathetic look. "You'll rip her apart on cross-examination."

Frank took a deep breath and cracked his knuckles. "I hope so, because if the jury believes her bullshit, she'll walk out of the courtroom a free woman. Ever since the trial started, every night I've dreamed of a guilty verdict and her being taken from the courtroom in handcuffs and sent away to prison."

The waitress brought their drinks back to the table and set them down. Beth and Frank picked up their drinks and swallowed a needed dose of relaxation. Frank sat his drink down and said quietly, "I'm going to the men's room."

Beth nodded and smiled as Frank walked toward the brick stairs up to the main section of the restaurant. A few bright rays of sun shined through the bamboo shoots and reminded Beth of the rapidly approaching sunset.

Beth's mother had always believed the last of the sunset was a very special time. She believed that five minute period of time between when the bottom of the sun hit the horizon, and the sun disappeared over the horizon, she could communicate with her dead relatives. She would always watch the sunsets and claim she silently talked with her dead relatives and they would wish her words of encouragement. When the sun disappeared over the horizon, she would always whisper, "Bye, bye."

Beth's parents had both died when she was a young lawyer and she missed them terribly. Whenever she watched a sunset, she always thought about her mother's superstitious belief of being able to communicate with relatives. Beth was not a believer, but in the past few years, she caught herself thinking of her mother at sunset more often.

Chapter 14

Judge Bronson looked at the jury. "Good morning, ladies and gentleman, I hope you had a restful night. It's time for the Defense to start their case." Judge Bronson looked at Amanda and said politely, "Please call your first witness."

"The Defense calls Lacy Turner," Amanda announced proudly.

There was a quiet stirring in the courtroom as everybody shifted their focus to Lacy. She was wearing a loose-fitting black dress that was tight at the collar and went down to her calves. She had on black pumps with no jewelry, and her long blonde hair was pulled back into a tight ponytail. She stood up and waivered for a second before she nervously walked to the witness stand. The clerk swore her in and Judge Bronson asked her to be seated. After she sat down, she looked at Amanda and forced a smile.

Frank was watching the jury closely to see how they reacted to Lacy's story. He was specifically looking for jurors making facial expressions doubting details of her story. He would make sure and hammer those points in cross-examination to reinforce the jurors' disbelief in her story.

Amanda asked pleasantly, "Please give us your name and address?"

Lacy cleared her throat and spoke distinctly. "My name is Lacy Turner and I live on Lely Boulevard in Naples, Florida."

"Where did you grow up, Ms. Turner?"

Lacy looked at the jury. "I was born at the Naples Medical Center, but I lived in Everglades City until I went away to college in Gainesville."

Amanda could tell Lacy was nervous, so she asked her an easy question. "What hobbies did you have when you were growing up?"

Lacy pondered her answer for a second. "My mom introduced me to swimming, but I got bored with it as I got older. My favorite thing was to go fishing with my dad in the backcountry of the Everglades, and I still go fishing as much as I can."

Amanda decided it was time to get some sympathy from the jury. "Do your parents still live in Everglades City?"

Lacy's eyes got wide and she stared in disbelief at Amanda for a moment before she started to tear up and instinctively looked down. After a few uncomfortable seconds, Lacy cleared her throat and answered softly, "They both died in a car wreck on Interstate 75 three years ago."

"I'm sorry," Amanda said gently.

Frank looked over at the jury, and they all looked sympathetically toward Lacy. Frank secretly cursed Amanda's skillful manipulation of the jury's feelings toward Lacy.

Amanda gave Lacy a few seconds to regain her composure before she asked, "What do you do for a living, Ms. Turner?"

Lacy gathered herself together and sat up in her chair before she answered. "I'm a psychologist in Naples, and I work for myself in private practice."

"Where did you go to college and graduate school?"

Lacy smiled. "I went to undergrad and grad school at the University of Florida. Go Gators!"

Frank noticed that three of the jurors smiled, and he wasn't happy. Amanda was doing a good job of trying to make Lacy likeable by the jurors. Of course, if jurors liked a defendant, then they were more likely to believe their story and acquit.

Amanda asked pleasantly, "How long have you been a practicing psychologist?"

Lacy considered her answer for a moment. "I'm just starting my fourteenth year in practice in Naples."

Amanda cocked her head to her left and lowered her voice. "When did you first meet the missing lady in this case, Patricia Hendricks?"

Lacy smiled at the fond memory. "Patricia and I met during our freshman English class at U.F."

"When did you first meet the victim of the murder in this case, Susan Kelly?"

Lacy looked down and put her left hand over her mouth for a couple of seconds. After she gained her composure, she looked up and answered flatly. "I met Susan at a fraternity party my first week at U.F., and we became friends."

Amanda held her hands out to her side. "Did you introduce Susan and Patricia to each other after this?"

Lacy nodded and smiled. "Yes. We lived in the same dormitory, so we had most of our meals together in the cafeteria, and we partied on the weekends. We became very close friends and moved in together as roommates in an off campus apartment our sophomore year. We lived together the rest of our time at college and became great friends."

Amanda looked at her notes. "Did you work during college?"

Lacy nodded. "Yes. I worked as a waitress at Hooter's during college and grad school."

"Did Susan and Patricia work during college?"

Lacy leaned back and considered her answer for a moment. "Patricia worked part-time at the campus library on the weekends. Susan's dad was a stockbroker and always gave her plenty of money, so she didn't have to work."

Amanda held her right hand toward the jury. "Could you

tell the jury how all three of you got your college nicknames, the Hooker, the Dancer and the Nun?"

Lacy smiled wistfully. "That was such a fun night when Susan and Patricia got their nicknames. We'd been at a frat party and we'd met some cool guys and partied with them. One of the guys suggested we all get something to eat at Denny's, so we piled into his car and went there. While we were eating, we all started talking about where we'd come from and what we liked doing. I'd talked about how I liked to go fishing back home and missed hooking the big ones. I told them how one of my co-workers at Hooter's had nick-named me a Hooker because I told her I missed hooking snook and tarpon back home in the Everglades.

"Well, the guys asked Susan what she liked to do, and she said she missed all the dance clubs in South Beach, so one guy named her the Dancer. One of the guys asked Patricia what she liked doing, and she was embarrassed and said she didn't get out much. Susan was drunk and chimed in and said, 'Let's call her the Nun because she's still a virgin.' All the guys snickered and Patricia was embarrassed, but she was a good sport about it. So, from that night forward, we were the Hooker, the Dancer and the Nun."

Amanda nodded and looked at the jury for a second before she continued, "Have you and Patricia stayed in touch since college?"

Lacy smiled. "Oh yes. We talked on the phone at least

once a week, and we'd probably take a girls' weekend two or three times a year. She was a schoolteacher—she always had the holidays off and long summer breaks—so she had time for girls' weekends. That is . . . at least until she married David."

Amanda crossed her arms. "Tell me about David Brennan."

Lacy shook her head and said bitterly, "His family owned a bunch of jewelry stores throughout the Southeast, and he helped them out as little as possible, but he was really just a trust fund baby. He was very controlling of Patricia and he was physically and emotionally abusive to her. He was such a weasel!"

Amanda looked at her notes for a moment and back at Lacy. "Patricia's nickname in college was the Nun. Did she have many boyfriends before she met David?"

Lacy smiled and blushed slightly. "Before David, she was always very careful about who she dated, and she didn't lose her virginity until she was 24. She'd only had two serious boyfriends before she started dating David at 30 and married him a year later. He treated her like a princess until he married her, and that's when the abuse started. She told me she'd never have kids with him because she didn't want to have that permanent connection with him."

Amanda looked down at her notes for a few seconds before she asked, "Have you and Susan had ups and downs in your friendship since college?"

Lacy slowly nodded and took a deep breath. "That's the understatement of the year," she said remorsefully.

"During your interview with the detective, were you truthful when you talked about the problems you and Susan had?

Lacy nodded forcefully. "Yes, I was truthful even though it was extremely embarrassing to talk about all those things from the past with a total stranger. I was scared that Susan was dead, Patricia was missing, and I was the only one left with Susan's blood all over me. I didn't want to tell any lies and make things look worse than they already did."

Amanda waited for a few seconds before she asked sympathetically, "How'd you feel when your texts and Facebook private messages were displayed on the screen during the trial?"

"I was humiliated," Lacy said softly. "Those were private thoughts and angry rants that I'd deleted. I had no idea that deleted things could be retrieved by computer experts."

Amanda pointed at Frank and raised her voice. "The prosecutor thinks these 15 exhibits show your motive to murder Susan. Did you slice your friend's neck and watch her bleed to death?"

Lacy sat up in her chair and said forcefully. "I did not kill Susan!"

Amanda pointed at Lacy and raised her voice. "If not

you, who killed her?"

"I don't know," Lacy pleaded passionately as she looked at the jurors. "I ask myself everyday who would do this. I don't know who did it."

Amanda waited for a few seconds and then asked. "Did Patricia do it?"

"Oh no, it's not possible." Lacy shook her head forcefully. "Patricia is not an angry or violent person. We always called her the 'peacemaker' because she always worked out the issues between Susan and me. She's the glue that held us together."

Amanda looked at her notes for a moment. "How'd you get the red marks around your wrists and ankles the night you were arrested?"

Lacy held her hands up to her side and shrugged. "I don't know. That day we'd all been at the beach on Cayo Costa, and I'd put lotion all over my body, and I didn't see any marks then. We also took cell phone pictures on the beach that day, and they show I didn't have any marks on my wrists or ankles."

Amanda pulled two eight by ten inch pictures from her notes on the podium and looked at Judge Bronson. "Your Honor, may I approach the witness to have her identify these two pictures?"

"Yes, you may." Judge Bronson said evenly.

Amanda walked to the witness stand and handed the two

pictures to Lacy. "Do you recognize Defense Exhibits 'C' and 'D'?"

Lacy looked at both pictures and nodded slowly. "I do. Exhibit 'C' is a picture Susan took of me sitting on a big piece of driftwood on the beach at Cayo Costa that day, and Exhibit 'D' is a blow up of the same picture."

"About what time was this picture taken?"

Lacy scratched her chin for a moment. "It was taken around 4:00 p.m. that day."

Amanda faced Judge Bronson. "Your Honor, I move Defense Exhibits 'C' and 'D' into evidence and ask that they be published to the jury."

"They will be so received," Judge Bronson said and pointed to the head bailiff. "Please give the pictures to the bailiff, and he'll show them to the jury."

Lacy handed the pictures to the head bailiff, who then walked over to the jury box and handed them to the closest juror. As the jurors looked at the pictures, Amanda returned to the podium and waited silently. Frank watched the jurors as they looked at the pictures, but they didn't show any emotions on their faces. One of the female jurors stared at Lacy for a few seconds after viewing the picture and looked at her wrists and ankles. After the jury had finished viewing the pictures, the head bailiff took the pictures to the clerk's table to be retained as evidence.

Amanda looked at Lacy. "Do you remember the arrest

173

pictures of you that was introduced into evidence by me earlier in the trial?"

Lacy nodded. "I do."

"Do you have any idea how those marks got on your ankles and wrists in those pictures?"

Lacy shook her head and said distressfully, "I have no idea."

Amanda held her hands out to her side. "Did you ever see Susan or Patricia smoke cigarettes?"

"No, never."

"Do you smoke cigarettes?"

"No, I never have."

"What hand do you write with?"

Lacy held up her left hand to her side. "I'm left-handed. I write with my left hand, and I golf and swing a softball bat with my left hand."

Amanda looked at her notes for a second and then looked back toward Lacy. "Whose idea was it to take a girls' weekend on the houseboat?"

"It was Patricia's idea." Lacy took a deep breath and spoke evenly. "She kept her 19-foot Boston Whaler at the marina and knew about the houseboat for rent there. She convinced us we all needed a girls' weekend of sun and fun, and we all agreed. It seemed like a great idea to get away."

"How long had Patricia's divorce been final before this?"

Lacy shrugged. "I think it'd been about three months

since the judge signed the order."

"How long had it been since Susan's divorce was final?"

"About eight months."

"Was it Susan's second divorce?"

Lacy nodded. "Yes. Her first marriage was to a body builder and lasted about four years. Her second marriage was to a surgeon and lasted for a little over eight years."

Amanda held her hands out to her side and asked playfully, "Did Susan ever tell you the difference between her first marriage and her second marriage?"

Lacy smiled and blushed. "She always said in her first marriage, the orgasms were real, but the diamonds were fake, and in her second marriage, those were reversed."

There were some snickers in the courtroom and three of the jurors smiled. Judge Bronson looked out in the audience area with a sly smile and said amusingly, "Everyone please keep your comments to yourselves."

Frank silently cursed Amanda and her skills humanizing Susan to the jury. She was consistently getting a few laughs and light moments from Lacy and making her seem incapable of a brutal murder. Frank knew he had his work cut out for him on cross-examination.

Amanda waited a few seconds for the courtroom to settle down before she continued. "Did you know anyone that was going to be staying at Cabbage Key that weekend?"

Lacy nodded. "I found out a few weeks before our girls'

weekend that some fishermen I knew were going to be at a snook fishing tournament at Cabbage Key, so we decided to anchor the houseboat there. I knew it was going to be mostly men at the tournament, so I figured we might meet some nice guys. We towed Patricia's boat behind the houseboat, and we used it to go to the beach at Cayo Costa first, and then Cabbage Key later that night. It seemed like the perfect weekend, but . . ." Lacy's voice trailed off and she put her face in her hands and started to weep.

After a few seconds of raw emotion and tears, Judge Bronson handed a box of Kleenex to Lacy. Lacy looked up and thanked her quietly as she set the box down in front of her, and pulled out two Kleenex. After she blew her nose, she took a deep breath and looked up at Amanda with red eyes.

Amanda asked sympathetically, "Let's start with renting the houseboat at Four Winds Marina. How'd all of you get to Four Winds Marina that day?"

Lacy cleared her throat. "Susan had driven over from Miami the night before, after she finished her afternoon aerobics class, and spent the night with me in Naples at my home. We got up early the next morning, drove to Patricia's house in Ft. Myers, loaded her luggage, and rode out to the marina together in my car."

"How long did it take to drive the houseboat to Cabbage Key and anchor up?"

Lacy scratched her chin as she considered her answer. "We left the marina around eleven in the morning and dropped anchor around one in the afternoon, so about two hours' cruise time."

Amanda stepped back from the podium and shrugged. "What happened after you anchored up?"

Lacy sat forward in her seat. "We put some beers and sandwiches in the cooler on Patricia's small boat and drove through Captiva Pass and into the Gulf. We drove a couple of miles north up the beach to where it was deserted and then anchored up near the shoreline in shallow water. We waded ashore and walked down the beach for a while, goofing off. That's where we took the pictures on the driftwood that were introduced as evidence. After that, we came back to the houseboat, got cleaned up and dressed for Cabbage Key. We cranked up the music on the houseboat and had a few drinks as we watched the sun set."

"How long was the boat ride from the houseboat to Cabbage Key?

Lacy shrugged. "About five minutes."

"What happened when you got to Cabbage Key?"

Lacy smiled slightly. "The party was already in full swing. They were having a snook tournament and had just finished the Captains' meeting explaining all the rules, and everybody was partying pretty hard in the bar. We walked in and saw some of my friends, and I introduced Susan and Patricia to them, and we all started having a good time. There were a lot of men and only a few women, so we enjoyed the attention. We were all recently divorced and definitely ready to start dating again."

Amanda cleared her throat and lowered her voice. "Did something happen later that night that upset you?"

Lacy nodded and answered bitterly. "It wasn't that big of a deal, but I'd been drinking, and I turned into a little drama queen. Susan started talking to one of my old boy-friends, and I got my feelings hurt. I pouted and ran my mouth and told Patricia she needed to take me back to the houseboat. Of course, Patricia wasn't going to leave Susan at Cabbage Key, so she gathered us all up and drove back to the houseboat, which was anchored about a half mile behind the docks in the basin. Patricia was the sober one—unfor-tunately, she was babysitting two drunks that were running their mouths. Once we got back to the houseboat, Susan and I had made up, and we opened up a bottle of tequila. Patricia was taking medication, so she didn't drink with us."

Amanda held out her hands. "How many shots of te-quila did you have?"

"I only remember two." Lacy shrugged and said softly, "I don't remember anything after that."

Amanda slowly scratched her chin before asking gently, "What do you remember next?"

Lacy ground her teeth for a second and closed her eyes

momentarily before she spoke emphatically. "I remember being shaken awake with flashlights in my face and men yelling at me to wake up."

"What did you do?"

"I put my hands in front of my eyes to shield the light and asked who they were, and what was going on."

"What were you told?"

"I was told, 'We're deputies here to arrest you for killing a woman.'"

"How'd you react?"

"I was in shock." Lacy shook her head. "I was drunk and disoriented, and didn't know who they were talking about. Then I looked down and saw blood all over me and I freaked out!"

Amanda raised her voice. "What happened next?"

Lacy's face grimaced. "I asked who was dead, and they gave me a dirty look. They picked up a bloody knife with gloved hands, and shoved it towards me and told me that I knew who I killed. I was handcuffed and pulled from the houseboat into the deputies' boat and they unzipped the body bag." Lacy put her left hand over her mouth and her voice broke as she continued in a raspy voice. "When I saw Susan, I threw up."

Lacy looked down and started weeping quietly. Amanda waited for Lacy to regain her composure before she continued. A short time later, Lacy grabbed a Kleenex, wiped her eyes, blew her nose, and then looked up at Amanda.

Amanda asked firmly, "What do you remember after that?"

Lacy shrugged her shoulders and said softly, "Everything on the boat after that is very blurry; I must've been in shock. I really don't remember many specifics until the interview at the Sheriff's Department."

Amanda pointed at Lacy and raised her voice. "Did you tell the truth to Detective Dagle?"

Lacy nodded emphatically. "I most certainly did."

Amanda looked at Judge Bronson. "May I approach the clerk, Your Honor, to get a piece of evidence?"

"You may," Judge Bronson responded flatly.

Amanda walked to the clerk's counter, lifted up the large clear baggie containing the murder weapon, turned to Lacy and held it up. "Had you ever seen this knife before the night of the murder when it was shown to you by the deputy?"

Lacy shook her head and said emphatically, "Absolutely not."

"Have you ever been in a Cabela's store?"

"Absolutely not. My father always supported the small businesses that sold bait and tackle in Everglades City. He raised me to stay out of chain stores like that and to support small businesses instead. I would never go to a Cabela's store."

Amanda set the knife down on the counter in front of the clerk and returned to the podium. She looked at her notes for a few seconds before she looked up and asked forcefully, "Did you kill Susan Kelly?"

Lacy leaned forward and looked anxiously at the jurors as she pleaded, "I did not kill Susan."

Amanda looked at Judge Bronson. "No further questions, Your Honor."

Judge Bronson looked at the jury. "This is a good time to break for lunch. I'll see you back here in an hour."

Chapter 15

Thursday, August 20, 2015 at 1:04 p.m.

Courtroom 6B, Lee County Courthouse in Ft. Myers, Florida

"You may cross-examine the witness, Mr. Powers."

Frank walked quickly to the podium with his notes. He was dressed in a dark green suit, with a starched white button down shirt and a yellow and white polka-dotted tie. After he set his notes down on the podium, he pointed at Lacy and asked boldly, "How did your fingerprints get on the murder weapon?"

Lacy instinctually leaned back in her chair before answering in a defensive tone, "I don't know."

Frank pointed at Lacy and asked loudly, "Wouldn't you agree with me that you must've touched the murder weapon to get your fingerprints on it?"

Lacy crossed her arms and tried to think of an answer that helped her. She finally responded tentatively, "My fingers must've touched the knife at some point because my fingerprints are on it. But, I don't know how, or when, I touched it. I've never seen that knife before the officer showed it to me. I just know I never could've sliced Susan's throat with a knife like that."

Frank pointed at Lacy and asked emphatically, "Isn't it possible that you killed Susan in a drunken rage, but you just don't remember?"

Lacy shook her head quickly and blurted out, "No! No, it's not possible!"

Frank looked over at the jurors, raised his eyebrows in disbelief, and dramatically shook his head. He turned back towards Lacy and asked forcefully, "How'd you feel in your senior year of college, when you found out your longtime boyfriend had gotten Susan pregnant?"

"I was hurt." Lacy looked mournful and lowered her voice. "I was angry and felt betrayed by both Susan and Jason."

Frank raised his voice. "How did you feel when you saw Jason here in court?"

Lacy's head snapped up and her face turned red. "I was livid! I hadn't seen him since college, and I see him for the first time in 18 years testifying against me in my murder trial. How would you feel?"

Frank looked toward Judge Bronson. "Objection, non-responsive. I'm asking Your Honor to instruct the witness not to answer my questions with questions."

Judge Bronson leaned forward and looked at Lacy. "Ms. Turner, please answer the questions succinctly, and don't add any questions back to the prosecutor."

Lacy nodded and said respectfully, "Yes, Your Honor. I apologize."

Judge Bronson looked toward Frank and nodded slightly. "Please continue your questions."

Frank felt exhilarated that he'd rattled Lacy and was determined to keep her on the defensive. He pointed at her and asked loudly, "How'd you feel when you saw your old boyfriend from grad school here in court?"

Lacy shrugged and said evenly, "Greg and I ended our relationship without too much drama. We've talked over the years, so it wasn't that uncomfortable to see him here."

"Did you enjoy that time in Key West at Fantasy Fest where Susan saw you with her ex-boyfriend, Greg?"

Lacy took a deep breath, contemplated her answer, and said flatly, "As I said in my interview with Detective Dagle, it was bittersweet. It was kind of satisfying to get a little revenge, but it was also sad to think about us not being friends like we once were."

Frank pointed his finger at Lacy. "How'd you feel when you were having sex with Susan's father?"

"Objection, argumentative," Amanda shrieked as she stood up.

Judge Bronson leaned forward and looked at the head bailiff. "Please take the jury to the jury room for a break. We'll resume in 10 minutes."

185

Everyone was on edge as the jury rose and walked into the jury room. Lacy's face was red and she sat up in her chair and glared at Frank. Frank and Amanda scowled at each other in mutual hatred. After the jury room door was shut, Judge Bronson looked at Frank and crossed her arms in frustration. "Mr. Powers, can you explain to me how you think that last question was proper?"

Frank was not backing down and said emphatically, "Your Honor, the defense put the Defendant's feelings at issue when they asked how she felt about those 15 texts and private Facebook messages in direct examination. Those 15 texts and private Facebook messages were from 2014 and 2015, about events in their senior year of college up until the night Susan Kelly was murdered. Based on the defense lawyer's questions of how the Defendant felt about these 15 texts and private Facebook messages, I'm allowed to inquire about how the Defendant felt from her senior year of college until the night of Susan Kelly's murder. This includes how she felt while having sex with the victim's father. They opened the door to this inquiry, and the rules of procedure allow me to ask questions about this. This is directly relevant to motive for the Defendant to murder the victim."

Judge Bronson leaned back in her chair and contemplated Franks' argument. After a few moments of serious contemplation, she looked over at Amanda, "What's the defense's response?"

186

Amanda shook her head and responded forcefully. "Your Honor, he's the one that introduced those 15 texts and private Facebook messages. According to the rules of evidence, I'm allowed to ask questions about the evidence that he introduces. That's what the rules of evidence contemplate and all of the cases interpreting the rules explain in detail."

Judge Bronson closed her eyes and leaned back in her chair for a few seconds as she contemplated her decision. She finally opened her eyes, leaned forward and crossed her hands in front of her on the bench before she spoke. "Counsel, I agree with both of your arguments. Both of you have made the Defendant's and victim's sex lives fair game for inquiry. What's good for the goose is good for the gander. Therefore, I'm making the ruling that you have both opened the door about each of their sex lives. So, you both can ask any questions you want about their feelings, motives, and revenge for all of their sexual escapades because it is relevant to the pending criminal charges."

Judge Bronson looked around the courtroom for a few seconds as she realized where this cross-examination was headed and sighed. She continued in an exasperated tone. "I would hope that counsel for both sides seriously consider the wisdom of asking detailed questions about sexual acts. Your jobs are to convince the jury of your positions, not to entertain them with salacious details of people's private lives. We're going to take a bathroom break for ten minutes, and

187

then I'm bringing the jury back in and resuming this trial. I hope both of you will think about my ruling and act with some restraint."

*   *   *   *   *

Judge Bronson looked warily at Frank and said politely, "Mr. Powers, please continue your cross-examination of the witness."

Frank pointed at Lacy and asked loudly, "Did you feel like you were getting revenge when you had sex with Susan's father?"

Lacy ground her teeth for a moment as she considered how to answer the loaded question. After a few seconds of contemplation, Lacy began her explanation of her indiscretion. "William and I had known each other for about 10 years, and he was always nice to me," Lacy said slowly and distinctly. "I obviously exercised poor judgment when I went back to his house, and I suppose that I was thinking it was a bit of revenge for Susan sleeping with Jason during college."

Frank stared at Lacy skeptically and tried to make her squirm. Lacy defiantly returned his stare, and there were five seconds of awkward silence in the courtroom before Frank looked down at his notes, and slowly shook his head in skepticism. Two of the male jurors in the back row looked at each other and winked. One of the female jurors on the front row raised her eyebrows and slowly shook her head.

Frank looked up and crossed his arms. "Why did you give an ultimatum to your business partner about dating Susan?"

Lacy gave a weary look and leaned forward. "That's really easy to answer—I've never liked mixing business and pleasure. I was very concerned that Dr. Moore would fall under Susan's spell and that when they broke up, he'd blame me. I enjoyed having fun with Susan, but I've seen her go through men like a lawnmower through grass. It wasn't a question of when Susan would dump him, only a question of how long, and how much money she could get out of him. I've seen it many times, and I didn't want my business to suffer because of her dating habits. Of course, my ultimatum caused our partnership to crumble, and I regret that. But, as we heard from Dr. Moore, my assessment of Susan's motives were correct."

Frank held his hands out to his side in a questioning manner and raised his voice. "How'd you feel yesterday when you heard your ex-husband confess to an affair with Susan?"

Lacy's face flushed and she glared at Frank for a few seconds. She took a deep breath and cleared her throat before she said bitterly, "It felt like a dagger going through my heart."

Frank looked down at his notes for a second and cleared his throat. "My notes show that the judge signed your divorce judgment on November thirteenth, two thousand fourteen. Is that correct?"

Lacy nodded. "That sounds about right."

"A few days after this is when you opened your mail and received a copy of the divorce judgment, correct?"

Lacy nodded. "Yes."

"Isn't it true, the same day you received the divorce judgment in the mail is when your ex-husband texted you about his affair with Susan in the past?"

Lacy whispered, "Yes."

"Isn't it true, you wanted to kill Susan when you found this out?"

Lacy looked down for a few seconds and shook her head slowly in frustration. She finally looked up, and her eyes were blood shot, her face pale. "I was mad as hell at both of them, but I didn't want to kill her."

"Isn't it true, six month later, Susan's throat was cut with a knife and your bloody fingerprints were on the knife?"

"Objection, argumentative!" Amanda said as she stood up quickly.

"Overruled," Judge Bronson said flatly and looked over at Lacy. "Please answer the question."

Everyone in the courtroom stared at Lacy. She sat back in her chair and instinctively crossed her arms for a few seconds before she spoke in a raspy voice. "Yes, that's true. But, I didn't kill her!"

Frank raised his eyebrows as he gave Lacy a small smirk. After a few seconds of silence, he turned toward Judge Bronson and said solemnly, "No further questions, Your Honor."

Judge Bronson looked at Amanda. "Does the Defense have any other witnesses?"

Amanda stood up wobbly. "No, Your Honor. The Defense rests."

Judge Bronson looked at the jury. "Ladies and gentleman, I'm sending you home for the day. The lawyers and I are going to stay here in the courtroom and review the jury instructions. I'll see you back here tomorrow morning at 9:00 a.m., at which time we will begin closing arguments. After closing arguments, you will retire to the jury room to begin your deliberations."

Chapter 16

Thursday, August 20, 2015 at 5:40 p.m.

Beth Mancini's home in Ft. Myers, Florida

Beth decided to go home and shower after work before she had dinner at Frank's condo. As she parked her Camry in her covered carport on the right side of her house, she wondered what kind of mood Frank would be in after the cross-examination of the Defendant. The carport was open on three sides but protected her car from the sun and rain. There were three cement steps to the kitchen door on the left side of the carport. The 50-foot Poinciana tree in front of her house provided shade and blossomed stunning red buds in the early summer. As she got out of her car, she could smell the gardenias in bloom from her backyard and hear a cardinal chirping for her mate. One of her old divorce clients owned a lawn service and kept her yard in perfect condition. Beth loved returning to her peaceful home after spending all day at her office trying to solve other people's problems. A nice warm bath, shaved legs, and a glass of wine would put her in the mood for a romantic evening. Her cats also needed some love before she left to see Frank.

Beth had only been in love four times in her life. Her first love was her high school sweetheart, and that relationship had ended when they went away to different colleges. Her second love was her first husband, but the marriage only lasted two years. She was single from 25 to 39 and had dated some nice men, but never fell in love. Her third love was her second husband and that lasted six years. Beth didn't date for a year after her second divorce. She dated a few men after that, but made no emotional connection until Frank came along, and now he was the fourth love of her life. She hoped he would be the last.

*　*　*　*　*

Beth walked up to Frank's door and heard his favorite CD playing on the stereo—Sinatra's Greatest Hits. When she first met Frank, she thought it was a little old fashioned, but it had grown on her, and she'd learned that Sinatra's music usually meant great sex. Sinatra's music had an immediate effect on her body, just like Pavlov's dog responding to stimuli. She quickly rang his door bell and giggled quietly to herself as she felt a warm glow forming rapidly all over her body.

Frank opened the door with a scotch in his hand and a smile on his face. "You're the best thing I've seen all day."

Beth stepped forward and gave him a warm, inviting kiss as she hugged him. "Glad to see you too. I've been thinking about you all day."

As they walked to the kitchen, Frank asked, "Wine or vodka?"

"I already had two glasses of wine at the house, so I'll stick with wine."

Frank nodded. "I stopped at Publix and got us a chicken Caesar salad and a loaf of garlic bread. How does that sound?"

"Perfect."

Frank poured Beth a glass of wine and asked, "How was your day?"

Beth smiled. "I had lunch with Gayla Stough. She's an old divorce client that's thinking about getting married again to a rich guy, but he wants a pre-nup. She wanted to pick my brain about it, so we met for lunch at the Veranda and discussed the issues."

Beth fondly remembered Gayla Stough's divorce and the good settlement she helped secure for her. Gayla was a trophy wife that was lucky enough to marry a rich man without a prenuptial. After eight years of marriage, Gayla's husband became impotent and Gayla promptly hired Beth to file for divorce. At the mediation six months later, they were $100,000 apart after four hours of negotiations and the parties were separated in different rooms. The mediator told

Beth that Gayla's husband said the case could settle if Gayla would talk to him privately. Gayla reluctantly agreed, but asked Beth to wait outside the door in case she had a question. Gayla's husband came down the hall to Gayla's room, smiled at Beth and went inside. After a minute together, Gayla came out and shut the door quietly as she looked at Beth and blushed.

Gayla whispered, "He said he'd give me the $100,000 if he could kiss my boobs for ten minutes." Gayla looked down the hall to make sure no one was listening and asked, "What do you think I should do?"

Beth arched her eyebrows and said wryly, "I'm sure you've done worse for less."

Gayla thought for a second and nodded. "Stand at the door and don't let anybody in," she whispered.

During the next ten minutes, Beth calculated Gayla was being paid $600,000 dollars an hour for her time. That was certainly better than Beth's hourly rate.

*   *   *   *   *

Beth took a drink of her wine and asked Frank, "How was the trial today?"

"The only witness they put on was the Defendant, and she was on the stand until about 3:00 p.m. After that, the Defense rested, and the judge sent the jury home. We spent

196

about an hour going over jury instructions and the verdict form. We've got closings tomorrow morning at nine, so I'm going to get up early and go over my notes. It's been a very stressful week, but tomorrow is show time."

Beth cocked her head to her right and asked, "So, how did Lacy do on the stand?"

Frank slowly shook his head and said wearily, "She did better than I thought she would. On direct, she was pretty convincing, but I drew a little blood on cross this afternoon. The whole case is about credibility and who do you believe." He shrugged and continued in a wary voice, "But, you never know what a jury thinks about everything until the verdict."

They were quiet for a few seconds and both took a drink as they thought about the trial. Beth asked, "What's your favorite closing argument about credibility of witnesses?"

Frank thought for a moment and chuckled to himself. "I think it would've been a murder trial I had a few years back. My only eye witness against the Defendant shooting the victim was a prostitute, and the defense brought in a thief and a drug dealer as alibi witnesses to refute her testimony. They testified the Defendant was with them at their house at the time of the murder, so he couldn't have killed the victim. So, the entire closing argument was about credibility and who should the jurors believe. I argued, 'You have a thief and a drug dealer that tell one story and a prostitute that tells a different one. Who do you believe? Always believe the prostitute because she works hard for a living.' The jury agreed with me and convicted."

Beth belly laughed. "I love your honesty! That must be why you win so many of your cases."

Frank smiled. "I learned a long time ago that jurors can see through bullshit."

Beth picked up her wine and pointed towards the lanai. "Let's go outside and watch the sunset."

Frank picked up his scotch. "Sounds good to me."

They walked out on the lanai and sat down in the cushioned chairs as Beth asked, "How did Lacy react when you asked her about her husband's affair with Susan?"

Frank snickered and nodded slowly. "I definitely got under her skin. But," Frank held up his right pointer, "she was also honest with the jury, and admitted it made her a little bit crazy. They seemed to be listening intently to her story. This jury is hard to read."

Beth said bitterly, "I can identify with affairs making you crazy."

Frank was quiet for a few seconds and took a healthy drink of his scotch as he silently debated whether he should ask his next question. His curiosity finally won out, and he asked sympathetically, "What was your first husband like before he cheated on you?"

Beth took a deep breath before answering and looked out to the river as she spoke. "We met in college at Mercer, and he was there on a baseball scholarship, but he took his studies very seriously. He was a very smart guy and was on the dean's list every semester. For pleasure reading, he'd always read three or four books at once; that's something I could never do. He was good looking, funny and smart, and I was in love. I thought I'd spend the rest of my life with him," Beth's voice quivered. "But I was wrong. He cheated on me in law school and got a co-worker pregnant."

"Oh, Honey, I'm sorry; I shouldn't have asked . . ." Frank's voice trailed off as he leaned back in his chair.

Beth waived her hand dismissively and shook her head as she took a long sip of wine. "That's when I decided to be a divorce lawyer," she quipped, smiling wistfully at Frank.

Frank waited for a few seconds before he ventured further. "What was your second husband like before he cheated on you?"

Beth wiped a tear away from her left eye and looked toward the sunset before she answered pensively. "He was tall, dark and handsome. Imagine Antonio Banderas with a deeper voice and three inches taller. I met him when he was doing work on my house when I remodeled and I fell head over heels for him. I actually proposed to him."

Frank laughed. "Did you make him sign a pre-nup since you had more money?"

Beth shook her head. "I thought about it, but I figured it might jinx the marriage. Even though I knew there are studies showing marriages with pre-nups have a lower divorce rate."

"What?" Frank asked incredulously.

Beth nodded her head and continued, "When people talk about finances up front, and what each side expects out of the marriage, it helps both sides understand each other. Of course, many engagements are called off during negotiations of pre-nups, but the ones that actually get married are more likely to last than marriages without pre-nups."

Frank drained his scotch and put his glass on the table as he digested her information about pre-nuptials.

Beth smiled and asked jovially, "Okay, enough of my dirty laundry. What about you? Why haven't you ever married?"

Frank shrugged. "I guess I never met the right woman."

"Oh, come on. That's the prepared answer you've told me before, and probably every other woman that's ever asked. Tell me the real reason," Beth pleaded earnestly.

Frank considered his answer for a second and then leaned forward in his chair and put his hands together, cracking his knuckles. He finally said quietly, "When I was growing up, all of my neighbors and close family members got divorced. In my job, I've seen so many failed marriages at the courthouse and it's always kind of scared me. I always liked dating one woman at a time and I enjoy monogamy, but I've been scared of the life-ever-after commitment of marriage."

Beth nodded slowly. "As a divorce lawyer, I can appreciate that. I see my fair share of train wrecks every week in my office."

They both looked at the sunset and enjoyed the silent contentment between them for about a minute. Beth fondly thought of her mother and the way she used to love sunsets and her claimed communication with dead relatives.

Beth spoke softly, "I'm just glad that we're together as a couple."

Frank reached over and tenderly put his hand on top of her hand. "I thank God every day that he brought you into my life."

Chapter 17

Friday, August 21, 2015 at 9:07 a.m.

Courtroom 6B, Lee County Courthouse in Ft. Myers, Florida

After everyone sat down, Judge Bronson looked at the jurors. "Ladies and gentlemen, the State goes first with their argument and then the defense. After the defense lawyer has made her argument, the State is permitted to have a rebuttal argument." Judge Bronson turned to Frank and said respectfully, "You may proceed with closing arguments, Mr. Powers."

Frank walked to the podium and set down his notes. He was dressed in a navy blue suit with a starched white button down shirt and his power red tie, hoping to appeal to the patriotic tastes of the jurors. The stress of the trial had gotten to him, and he had dark circles under his eyes. A small fever blister was starting to form on his lower lip. He had not slept well the night before and looked exhausted. He looked at every juror momentarily before he spoke.

"Ladies and gentleman, I'd like to thank you for your time and attention during this trial. It's been a long week for all of us, and I want you to know that the State Attorney's Office and their representatives appreciates your dedication and service. Our judicial system depends on jurors to give their time and hear difficult cases and return fair verdicts."

Frank looked down at his notes and cleared his throat before he continued.

"Ladies and gentleman, I'd like to start with a simple question: 'Who was on the houseboat when Susan Kelly was murdered?'"

Frank looked each juror in the eye before he continued in a determined voice. "The Defendant said only the three women came back from Cabbage Key on Patricia Hendricks' 19-foot Boston Whaler. The manager from Cabbage Key followed them to the dock and saw all three women leave together and no one else. It is uncontroverted that the night Susan Kelly died, only three people came back to the house-boat from Cabbage Key. That was the last time that anybody ever saw the Hooker, the Dancer and the Nun all alive."

Frank turned and pointed at Lacy. "The Defendant admitted her last memory was Susan Kelly and her doing tequila shots on the houseboat while Patricia Hendricks abstained."

Frank stared at Lacy for another second before he turned and faced the jurors. "Ladies and gentlemen, since they were the only three people on the boat, there are only three possible explanations for who killed Susan Kelly. The first explanation is that Patricia Hendricks killed Susan Kelly while the Defendant was passed out and swam away, because her 19-foot boat was still tied up to the houseboat when the deputy arrived. However, even the Defendant states she doesn't think it's possible that Patricia Hendricks killed Susan Kelly."

Frank held up his right pointer. "The second explanation is Lacy Turner killed both women and threw them overboard. One was eaten by sharks, and the other body drifted in the water until a Good Samaritan called and reported the body floating in the water, and the police arrived on the scene."

Frank shrugged and changed his tone of voice to sarcastic. "The third explanation is that an unknown person drove up to the houseboat, killed Susan Kelly while Lacy Turner slept, and then kidnapped Patricia Hendricks and took her away to parts unknown. Of course, no one ever sent a ransom note to prove that Patricia Hendricks was kidnapped."

Frank shook his head slowly for a few seconds and changed his tone back to normal. "Ladies and gentlemen, Judge Bronson will instruct you on the law before you begin your deliberations. She'll tell you that the State has the burden of proof in the case, and we have to prove our case to you, beyond all reasonable doubt, before you can find the Defendant guilty of the charge.

"I suggest to you that the evidence in the case points

to only one explanation—Lacy Turner killed her longtime romantic rival in a drunken rage. She either doesn't remember it because of the amount of alcohol she consumed, or she remembers, but has made up this story to avoid responsibility for her actions.

"We've shown you that Lacy Turner's fingerprints were on the bloody murder weapon, which was found approximately two feet from her by the responding deputy. We've shown you that the victim's blood was all over the Defendant. And," Frank raised his right pointer finger before he continued, "we have shown you 15 texts and private Facebook messages between the Defendant and the victim, which show the motives Lacy Turner had to kill her old college roommate, Susan Kelly. I did not take pleasure in bringing out all of the sordid history between the victim and the Defendant. However, it was important to show you the motive that drove the Defendant to commit such a gruesome murder.

"There's overwhelming evidence that shows what drove Lacy Turner to kill, and we've shown that Lacy Turner was drunk enough that night to drown her inhibitions. Her drunkenness allowed her brain to think of how to get rid of her biggest romantic rival, someone that she perceived to have wrecked her life with her college sweetheart. In her own words, 'he was the one that I'd marry, have kids with, and live happily ever after.' But, her dream life never happened because of Susan Kelly sleeping with her boyfriend."

Frank hesitated and again held up his right pointer finger. "She acted on her most secret fantasy and she killed Susan Kelly in cold blood!"

"Objection!" Amanda shouted out as she stood up. "There is zero evidence that Lacy Turner had any fantasy to kill Susan Kelly!"

Judge Bronson held up her right pointer toward Amanda. "Objection overruled, counselor. This is closing argument and the prosecutor can make arguments that are related to the evidence. Of course, when it's your turn, you may do the same." Judge Bronson turned to Frank and lowered her voice. "Please continue your argument, counselor."

Frank took a deep breath before he continued in a calm voice. "I'm not going to spend a lot of time here in closing argument stating the obvious – Lacy Turner killed her romantic rival in a drunken rage and passed out after the brutal murder. I'd ask that you return a guilty verdict after your deliberations."

As Frank returned to his table, Judge Bronson looked at Amanda. "Does the Defense wish to make a closing argument?"

Amanda rose quickly and nodded. "Yes, Your Honor."

Amanda was dressed in a dark blue dress, resting just over her knees, with a traditional pearl necklace and bright red leather shoes with four-inch heels. It was a bold fashion statement but still had a patriotic flare. Lacy was dressed blandly in a gray pantsuit and white blouse with her hair pulled back in a tight ponytail, no jewelry, and minimal makeup. Amanda had coached Lacy to dress extremely conservatively and not wear expensive jewelry during closing arguments so jurors wouldn't notice her looks before they began deliberations.

Amanda set her notes down on the podium and looked up at the jurors. "Ladies and gentlemen, Lacy and I thank you for your attention during this trial. I know it's been an imposition on your time, but our country's judicial system couldn't function without impartial jurors, such as yourselves. Since 1776, our great country has allowed individuals to challenge a government prosecutor's allegations in open court and let an independent jury decide guilt or innocence. It's a tremendous burden to have someone's life in your hands, but we've noticed you've paid close attention to all of the evidence that's been submitted for your consideration. At this time, I'd like to go over that evidence.

"Let's first talk about the strap marks on my client's wrists and ankles. What do we know for certain about those marks? We know those marks weren't there at 4:00 p.m. on the day of the murder."

Amanda looked at Judge Bronson. "May I approach the clerk and retrieve the pictures introduced into evidence, Your Honor?"

Judge Bronson nodded and said evenly, "You may."

Amanda walked over to the clerk's area and the clerk handed her the two pictures. Amanda returned to the podium and held one up in each hand and continued. "On my left is the picture of Lacy on a piece of driftwood, and on my right is the blowup of the same picture. All of you looked closely at these pictures earlier this week and you saw that there were no marks on Lacy's wrists, or ankles, immediately before the murder. You also saw the pictures of Lacy after she was arrested, and there were visible marks and bruising on both her wrists and ankles."

Amanda set the pictures down on the podium and held up her right pointer finger. "There were marks on the victim's wrists and ankles, but they were much more serious. You heard the medical examiner state that this indicated a struggle before the victim died. So, let's think about this. We know the victim's wrists and ankles were bound before she was tortured and her neck was sliced. We know Lacy tells us she doesn't remember what happened."

Amanda shrugged and raised her voice. "What does this show us? I submit that this shows both Lacy and Susan were bound before the killer decided to torture Susan, but because Lacy was passed out, she didn't struggle or witness the torture. After the killer finished torturing Susan and killed her, he put some blood on Lacy and then put the murder weapon in Lacy's hand, squeezing her fingers on the murder weapon to transfer her fingerprints. The killer then dropped it by her while she was passed out and left. He knew it would make Lacy look guilty. I have used the word 'he' when describing the real killer, but it could've been the real killer was a 'she'. We don't know for sure. All we know for sure is that Lacy couldn't have killed Susan if her hands and ankles were bound."

Amanda took a deep breath and looked at the jurors individually before she continued in a lower voice. "Who would do something like this? It could've been one of the drunk fishermen from the tournament that followed them back to the houseboat. Or it could've been the missing woman, Patricia Hendricks. We don't know, and we're not required to prove who did this terrible crime—the State has the burden of proving Lacy did this crime. If they can't prove beyond a reasonable doubt she did it, then your verdict must be not guilty. If you don't know who killed Susan, then the State hasn't proven it, and your verdict must be not guilty."

Amanda looked down at her notes for a moment and lowered her voice. "The next issue is the missing lighter that was used to torture the victim with burns to her nostrils and nipples. We know that none of the women smoked, so none of them had lighters. We also know that the water around the houseboat wasn't searched by divers for any evidence. I submit that the reason the lighter wasn't found is that the real killer was a smoker and took the lighter with him.

"Now, the prosecutor suggested that the grill lighter

could've been used. I submit that's not a reasonable explanation because the houseboat was dark that night, and the real killer would not have known that there was a random grill lighter somewhere on the houseboat." Amanda held up her right pointer finger before she continued, "And remember, the burden of proof is on the State. The State didn't even test to see if the grill lighter was in working condition. It was sitting out on a grill on a houseboat that's in salt water, and it could've been corroded and not in working order. If you don't know, then the State hasn't proven it. What else didn't the State do? They didn't check the grill lighter for fingerprint or DNA evidence. If you don't know, then the State hasn't proven it!"

Amanda was energized when she saw two female jurors on the front row slowly nodding during her argument. She raised her voice and continued, "What else didn't the State do? There was no blood work done on the victim or the Defendant. The coroner could've sent a blood sample to the lab to find out what drugs were in the victim's system, and how much alcohol was in her system. The same thing could've been done by Detective Dagle when interviewing Lacy. He could've gotten a blood sample to test for alcohol or drugs. Remember, Lacy said she didn't remember what happened. Did alcohol or drugs cause this memory lapse? We don't know because the State hasn't proven it with blood evidence!"

Amanda looked down at her notes and cleared her throat before she continued. "I'd like you to think back to the coroner's testimony about the fatal knife wound to the victim's neck. The medical examiner stated the entry and exit were consistent with someone that was right handed. You've observed Lacy writing notes all during the trial with her left hand and she testified she was left-handed. I submit to you that when people use knives, they use their dominant hand, so we know it wasn't Lacy that sliced Susan's neck."

Amanda walked to the side of the podium and continued in a lower voice. "Ladies and gentlemen, the prosecutor will get to have a rebuttal argument after I sit down and then Judge Bronson will give you instructions on the law and how you should conduct your deliberations. You'll hear that the State must prove their allegations against Lacy against all reasonable doubt. This means if you have a legitimate question about the evidence and you aren't satisfied that the State has met its burden, then you must return a not guilty verdict. It's not the Defendant's burden to prove she's innocent, so if you have questions about the evidence, then the conclusion must be that the State hasn't met its burden of proof beyond all reasonable doubt, and you must return a not guilty verdict. That's not just my opinion but the instructions that Judge Bronson will give to you before you begin your deliberations."

Amanda walked back behind the podium and continued

in a stronger voice. "I challenge the prosecutor to answer the following three questions: One, why did Lacy have marks around her wrists and ankles? Two, why were there burn marks on the victim's nostrils and nipples? Three, why didn't the 'Good Samaritan' that made the 911 call stay on scene and direct the police to the floating body?"

Amanda pulled out an eight by eleven inch piece of white paper with red ink script on it. She held it up and continued, "I don't want the prosecutor to forget to answer these questions, or ignore them, so I wrote all three of these questions down on a piece of paper, and I'm going to leave them on the podium so he can answer them when he gets up here. In fact, I challenge him to answer these questions."

Amanda turned to Judge Bronson and said respectfully, "The Defense rests, Your Honor."

Judge Bronson turned to Frank. "Does the State have a rebuttal argument?"

"Yes, Your Honor," Frank said calmly as he rose and walked to the podium. Every eye in the courtroom was on him when he picked up the piece of paper on the podium, walked to the defense table, laid it in front of Amanda, and returned to the podium. During this entire time walking in the courtroom, he never looked at Amanda or said anything to her.

Once he returned to the podium, he looked at the jury and said calmly. "I'm not going to respond to the 'piece of paper' trick that the defense lawyer used in her closing argument. The defense lawyer is simply trying to rattle me and hopes that I don't talk to you about the overwhelming evidence against her client."

Frank looked all of the jurors in the eyes before he continued in a reasoned tone. "We have proved motive. We have proved how the victim died and showed you that her blood was on the Defendant. We have proved the murder weapon was found two feet from the Defendant's hand, and her fingerprints were on the murder weapon. Quite simply, we have proved that Lacy Turner is guilty of murder, and I'm asking you to return a guilty verdict. Thank you for your time."

Frank turned to Judge Bronson and said confidently, "The State rests, Your Honor."

As Frank returned to his table, Judge Bronson looked at the jury. "At this time, we're going to take a 15 minute break before I instruct you on the law."

* * * * *

It was 11:20 a.m., and Judge Bronson had just finished reading her instructions on the law to the jury. She looked up at the jurors and said, "The first thing you should do when you retire to the jury room is to pick a jury foreman, and it can be a man or a woman. I'm giving you a piece of paper, a

214

pen, a copy of the jury instructions, and the verdict form. If you have a question, write it on a piece of paper and give it to the jury foreman, who will knock on the jury room door and notify the bailiff sitting outside your door. Once you've decided on a verdict, the jury foreman should check the correct spot on the verdict form and sign it. After that, knock on the jury door and let my bailiff know you've reached a verdict." Judge Bronson shifted in her seat and smiled. "On a lighter note, I've ordered a pepperoni pizza and a vegetarian pizza for your lunch while you deliberate. When they arrive, the bailiff will bring both of them, sodas, and water to you. At this time, you may retire to the jury room."

Chapter 18

Friday, August 21, 2015 at 5:07 p.m.

Courtroom 6B, Lee County Courthouse in Ft. Myers, Florida

Frank had texted Beth when the jury went out for their deliberations. After she finished returning her client's calls and working on research projects, she had walked over to the courthouse to check on Frank. After she went through the security at the front entrance, she took the elevator up to the sixth floor and walked by Amanda and Lacy sitting on a bench in the lobby outside the courtroom. They had both given her the evil eye, and she ignored them. There were three T.V. reporters talking on their cell phones and one newspaper reporter typing furiously on his laptop sitting on the other side of the lobby. Beth walked quietly past everyone and entered courtroom 6B.

Frank and the two bailiffs in the courtroom had been sitting at the prosecutor's table, talking quietly about sports. When Frank heard the courtroom door open, he turned in his swivel chair and saw Beth coming toward him. He stood up and said gently, "Hello, honey, how're you doing?"

"I'm tired, but not nearly as tired as you," Beth responded sympathetically.

Frank met her at the bar and squeezed her hand. "The jury's been out a little over five hours. The judge ordered some pizza and it got delivered for lunch, so I know they spent some time eating that. We should've had a verdict by now."

Beth cocked her head. "How about you? Did you eat anything?"

Frank motioned toward the bailiffs with his head. "These guys always have a stash in the back room. We ate some chips and granola bars a little while ago."

Both of the bailiffs rubbed their bellies in mock satisfaction. "Great chow," the head bailiff quipped.

Beth gave them a thumbs up and then looked at Frank. "Do you think they'll reach a verdict tonight or come back tomorrow and continue deliberations?"

Frank shrugged. "After the jury went out, Judge Bronson told us she was going to let them deliberate until six and then send them a note and ask them if they wanted to come back tomorrow."

*   *   *   *   *

At 5:32 p.m., there was a knock on the jury door, and the head bailiff went and opened it. He was handed a folded piece of paper and he shut the door quietly. As he walked by Frank sitting at the State's table, he whispered, "They have a note," and continued to the bailiff's office to make a call to the judge's chambers to alert her.

Beth said quietly, "What do you think?"

Frank paled. "I don't like it when the jury deliberates this long and hasn't reached a verdict."

Frank sat down and stared straight ahead as his stomach churned. Beth sat down on the front row and decided to be quiet while Frank mulled over what the question might be. It took about five minutes before the judge and everyone reassembled to their spots in the courtroom, and Frank just stared ahead and said nothing during this time. Sitting in the front row, directly behind Frank, Beth felt anxious because she'd never seen Frank like that before. She wanted to reach out and rub his back, but she knew it wasn't possible. Amanda and Lacy talked quietly between themselves at their table, and the television and newspaper reporters whispered their opinions about the note as they waited for court to resume. They finally heard a door shutting in the back hallway, which meant the judge was headed down the short hallway for the bench.

"All rise, Judge Alexandra Bronson is presiding over this court," the head bailiff announced stiffly.

Judge Bronson walked in, sat down, and looked around the court room. "Please be seated."

After everyone sat down, Judge Bronson said, "The bailiff has informed me that the jury has a note, so I'm going to bring the jury in and read it in open court. I want no loud reaction to the note here in court. If there's an outburst, I'll hold that person in contempt of court and send them to jail. If you can't control yourself, you need to leave the court-room at this time."

Judge Bronson looked around the courtroom to see if anyone wanted to leave, but no one moved. Judge Bronson looked at her head bailiff and nodded, "Bring in the jury."

All of the jurors walked slowly into the courtroom and didn't make eye contact with anyone. After they all sat down, Judge Bronson said solemnly, "Ladies and gentle-man of the jury, the bailiff has handed me a note from you, but I haven't read it yet. I will read it aloud here in court, so everyone can hear it at the same time." Judge Bronson unfolded the note, read it silently and looked perplexed for a moment. She cleared her throat after a few seconds and spoke distinctly, "The notes says: Judge Bronson, We are hopelessly deadlocked. Half of us are convinced the Defen-dant is guilty, and the other half is convinced the Defendant is not guilty. We can't agree on a verdict. What do we do?"

Judge Bronson leaned back in her chair and considered her answer for a few seconds as people in the courtroom shifted in their seats and looked at each other in confusion. There was total silence in the courtroom as everyone stared at the jurors in disbelief. All of the jurors looked down to avoid the inquisitive looks.

Judge Bronson leaned forward and said sincerely, "Ladies and gentlemen of the jury, it's very hard for a jury to reach a unanimous verdict, and sometimes, it's impossible to reach a unanimous verdict. This looks like one of those times. When a jury can't reach a verdict, it's called a hung jury, and I'm required by law to declare a mistrial." She took a deep breath and continued. "Therefore, at this time, I declare a mistrial. The parties will come back at a later time, and we will have a second trial with a different jury. I want to thank you for your service this week, and I'm discharging you at this time. The bailiff will escort you to your cars."

Chapter 19

Friday, September 11, 2015 at 10:00 a.m.

Three weeks after the trial in Beth Mancini's law office

Beth was talking to a client on the phone when her paralegal walked in and handed her a note that read: *Your ex-client, Patricia Hendricks a/k/a the Nun, is in the waiting room and wants to talk with you!*

Beth almost dropped the phone as she read the note and her mind started swirling with the possibilities. She told her client she had an emergency and had to call her back. After she hung up, she rushed out of her office into her waiting room. There she saw Patricia sitting on her red leather couch wearing jeans and a button up pink blouse with white tennis shoes. Beth noticed her hair was cut much shorter and had been dyed red.

Beth held her arms open and stepped forward. "Give me a hug! I thought you'd been eaten by sharks!"

Patricia's face blushed and she stood up and gave Beth a long, heartfelt hug. After they separated, Patricia asked quietly, "Can we talk in your office?"

Beth nodded and walked back into her office with Patricia following behind her in an awkward silence. As Patricia walked toward a chair in front of Beth's mahogany desk, Beth closed her door as her paralegal gave her quizzical looks from the hallway. Beth wondered what to say as she walked silently from the door to her swivel leather chair behind her desk.

Beth sat down and gave Patricia a sympathetic smile for a second, and then asked gently, "What happened?"

Patricia leaned back in her chair and sighed quietly before she began. "I'm not proud of myself for what happened. But, I want you to know that I never meant for anybody to get hurt."

Beth nodded as she responded tentatively, "I believe that. But you've got to tell me exactly what happened so I can help you."

"That's why I'm here; I don't know what to do," Patricia answered in flustered tone. "You remember my ex-husband, David Brennen? You remember how possessive and abusive he was? Remember at mediation, when David said I was his forever, because I was his wife forever?"

Beth readily agreed and nodded. "I remember how David refused to acknowledge the divorce process. He wouldn't even agree the marriage was irretrievably broken; we had to go to trial on that issue, alimony, and dividing up all the property. He even wanted you to return to him all of your jewelry and your car back that was purchased during the marriage. He wouldn't agree to any alimony, after a nine year marriage, or give you any of the property acquired during the marriage. He was a world class asshole. But, the judge made a fair ruling, giving you what you were entitled to."

Patricia looked down and was quiet for a few seconds before she said softly, "I was convinced that David would never leave me alone. Do you remember him following me down the hallway at the courthouse after trial until the bailiffs came up and made him leave me alone?"

Beth nodded and said compassionately, "Yes, I do. I was very happy when your divorce was final, and you could finally get away from him."

"That's the problem," Patricia lamented. "I knew David would never leave me alone unless he thought I was dead."

Beth was perplexed. "What do you mean by that?"

Patricia cleared her throat and sat up in her chair. "I made up a plan to disappear and fake my drowning, so he'd think I was dead."

Beth shook her head slowly. "I don't understand."

Patricia considered her words before she spoke. "You have to understand I didn't know how Susan died—until yesterday."

Beth was troubled, but decided she needed to reassure her client so she would speak freely. "Patricia, you're my client, and anything you tell me is privileged. That means you can tell me everything that happened that night without being worried about what I think or who I might tell. I'm not allowed to divulge anything you tell me, to anybody, without your permission. It's called attorney/client privilege. Do you understand?"

Patricia nodded. "Yes, I understand," she said softly. Patricia lifted her shoulders up, took a deep breath, smiled and said confidently, "It was my idea to have the girls' week-end on the houseboat so I'd have witnesses to my disappear-ance."

Beth cocked her head to the left, and after a few mo-ments of clarity, asked quizzically, "How did you do it?"

Patricia smiled and said, "I told the girls I couldn't drink because I was on medication. When they came back to the houseboat after partying on Cabbage Key, I suggested they have tequila shots to help them make up from their fight in the bar. When I poured the shots, I put ruffies in them, so they'd pass out while I did my disappearing act from the houseboat."

Beth shook her head. "What are ruffies? The date rape drug?"

"Yes. The slang name for ruffies is the 'date rape' drug, but the scientific name is flunitrazepam. It causes people to pass out and have memory loss from when it gets in their system."

Beth crossed her arms and tried to hide her disapproval. "Oh yeah, I've heard of those. So, what happened on the houseboat after you spiked their drinks?"

Patricia shrugged. "After two tequila shots, they were both passed out—Susan outside on the deck in a folding lounge chair, and Lacy inside on the couch. That's when I called my cousin on his cell phone and asked him to come get me in his johnboat. He'd seen me with black eyes during the marriage and he knew David was dangerous, so he'd agreed to help me. I had bought a disposable phone from Walmart so the call to my cousin couldn't be traced to my cell phone number. He was waiting in his truck at the kayak landing area near Tarpon Lodge on Pine Island. It was about a 15 minute ride for him in his johnboat to come get me on the houseboat. I told him to use the kayak landing because there'd be no witnesses there at night, and we could load his boat in the back of the truck and leave quietly. When we left the houseboat, they were both passed out, but they were fine."

Beth stared at Patricia in disbelief.

Patricia took a deep breath before she continued. "My plan was for them to wake up in the morning with me missing. I assumed everyone would think I fell overboard and drowned, and my body was eaten by sharks."

Beth sat back in her chair and held her hands out to her side. "What did you do when you got back to your cousin's truck?"

Patricia nodded slowly and answered in a hard tone. "I had a plan in place from that point on. He drove me to the Naples airport where I'd chartered a private plane, in a different name, to take me to Costa Rica, and the pilot was waiting on me in the pilot's lounge. Once I was in Costa Rica for a few days, I chartered another plane, in a different name, to take me to Belize, and that's where I've been living under an assumed name since then. I planned on staying there forever and starting a new life."

Beth stood up and walked over to her window, and stared at the people walking down the sidewalk as she tried to understand her client. After a few seconds, she turned around and looked at Patricia. "Why did you do all of this?"

Patricia shook her head slowly and said wistfully, "David never would've left me alone. If he thought I'd drowned and been eaten by the sharks, he wouldn't look for me, and I'd be free."

Beth slowly digested Patricia's story for a few seconds as she sat back down at her desk. "What did you think when you heard about Susan being killed and Lacy charged with murder?"

"I saw it online because I read the local paper's digital edition everyday while I was away." Patricia scratched her chin and slowly shook her head. "I didn't know what to think at first. I couldn't imagine that Lacy would've killed

Susan, but the story in the paper made it look bad for Lacy. I kept reading all the articles and following the trial, but I couldn't ever make up my mind if she really did it."

Beth held her hands out to her side and asked sharply. "What did you think about the verdict?"

Patricia grinned slightly and spoke softly. "I was relieved, because in my heart, I knew Lacy couldn't have killed Susan."

Beth was baffled by Patricia's story, and leaned back in her chair for a few seconds to process everything she just heard. "So, if your plan had worked so well, why did you come back to Ft. Myers?"

Patricia cocked her head and looked surprised. "Didn't you see the news two days ago? I saw it online that David was killed by his new girlfriend, in self-defense, when he was beating her at her apartment."

Beth shook her head. "No, I don't normally watch the news. It's too depressing."

Patricia nodded. "Apparently, they were both drunk, and David had hit her a bunch of times because he accused her of flirting with a man at a bar. She'd had enough and grabbed a kitchen knife and stabbed him 27 times. All of the neighbors heard the screaming and called 911. When the cops arrived, he was dead, but she'd been beaten pretty badly before that. She had two black eyes and four broken ribs, so they believed her claim of self-defense and didn't arrest her."

"Wow! What a way to die," Beth quipped. "I can't say I'm surprised, though."

"Karma's a bitch," Patricia said dryly.

Beth nodded, but didn't say anything.

Patricia continued bitterly, "All of those times he slapped me around because he thought I was looking at another man, and I wasn't. I just took it and never called the cops."

Beth cleared her throat. "So, you came back because you don't feel threatened now?"

Patricia straightened up in her chair and slowly shook her head. "The real reason I came back was to get his laptop from his house before anybody took it. He always liked to make amateur porn videos of us having sex, and he saved all of the videos on his laptop. I didn't want anyone to get those videos and post them online, so I came back to get the laptop before one of his relatives got it. They were as bad as him, so I'm certain they would have posted them online just for the sport of it."

Beth leaned back in her chair and shook her head slowly before she asked, "Did you get it?"

Patricia smirked and said proudly, "It was actually very easy. He thought I'd died, so he never changed the locks on his house. I used my key to get in yesterday afternoon and found his laptop on the kitchen table. I put it in a bag and went back to my hotel room to look at it."

"Where's the laptop now?"

"I've got it locked in the trunk of my rental car downstairs."

Beth asked slowly, "So, did you find the video collection?"

Patricia looked down and ground her teeth for a second before she spoke wearily. "I found all of his porn collection—me and all of his other women over the years that he filmed. But, while I was going through his laptop, I found a video file titled, 'Houseboat Night.'"

The hair on the back of Beth's neck rose up. "Did you open it?"

Patricia's face turned white and she answered bitterly, "I opened it. It was a GoPro video of him . . . torturing . . . and killing Susan."

Beth was silent and felt sick to her stomach. She instinctively lifted her left hand up to her mouth and started biting her pinky nail. After she gathered her thoughts, she asked quietly, "What's a GoPro video?"

Patricia raised her right hand to her forehead, and held her thumb and pointer finger about two inches apart. "It's a small camera that's mounted on a band that goes around your forehead. The camera sees things from the same vantage point as your eyes, and records everything you see and say. That's what people use to film their action videos that they post online with YouTube and Facebook."

Beth grimaced and whispered, "Do you mean there's a

video of the murder?"

A single heavy tear ran down Patricia's left cheek and she nodded slowly. "It's a video that he proudly narrates."

Chapter 20

Friday, September 11, 2015 at 11:10 a.m.

The State Attorney's Office in Ft. Myers, Florida

Frank walked quickly into his office lobby and saw Beth and Patricia sitting anxiously on the edge of their chairs. Patricia was holding a closed laptop to her chest and had red swollen eyes. Beth's face was pale and she looked distraught, but she managed a weak smile to Frank.

Frank motioned toward his office and said solemnly, "Let's go back to my office and talk."

After they all silently walked down the hallway to Frank's office, he pointed to chairs and closed the door as they sat down. Patricia sat her laptop on the edge of Frank's desk and leaned back in her chair. He walked around his desk and sat down while staring incredulously at Patricia.

Frank cleared his throat and looked at Beth as he spoke in his official voice. "In your phone call to me, Ms. Mancini, you said that you and your former client needed to meet with me because you had important information about the murder of Susan Kelly."

Beth nodded and looked at Patricia. "Tell Mr. Powers what you told me."

Patricia repeated her story for Frank, who sat and listened in total amazement. After Patricia finished her description of everything that had happened, she stared at the laptop sitting on Frank's desk for a few seconds.

Frank was stone-faced and pointed to the laptop as he said in astonished tone, "Let's watch the video."

Patricia opened the laptop and scrolled through the files until she found "Houseboat Night" and hit play. They all watched:

The Go-Pro video showed the inside of a flats boat, dimly lit by lights from the control panel on the console, and a single low wattage light on the side of the console, angled down by a cover, to prevent night blindness for boaters. The boat moved through the water at a high rate of speed. A hand reached out, slowly pulled the throttle back, the outboard engine noise decreased, and the boat quietly settled into the water. The hand moved down, turned the key to the off position, and the outboard engine stopped running. It was total silence for a second.

David Brennan said, "This should be a fun night. I had my private investigator hide a GPS tracking device inside Patricia's boat, so I can monitor wherever her boat is. I was at home today and saw the damn boat was behind Cabbage Key, next to Cayo Costa, so I figured she was trying to have some quiet time away from everyone, and it ain't gonna happen, bitch! I'm gonna sneak up on her with my trolling motor and take care of her once and for all. I'll be damned if I'm going to keep paying alimony to that bitch."

The video showed David walking to the front of his flats boat and putting the trolling motor into the water. He turned on the trolling motor, and started moving forward slowly and quietly. All of the running lights on the boat had been turned off and there was a quarter moon about 25 degrees above the horizon. David pulled out a cigar and cutter from his left shirt pocket, cut the cigar, and put the cutter back in his pocket. He pulled a butane torch cigar lighter from his right pants pocket and lit the cigar. The flame on the end of the cigar glowed strong as he inhaled and put the lighter back in his pocket. The boat moved quietly toward some lights in the distance. After a few minutes of heading toward the lights in near silence, they become more distinct and brighter, and the outline of a houseboat and a smaller boat tied off the stern of the houseboat became visible.

David said quietly, "It looks like the bitch decided to rent a houseboat for the weekend. I guess I should get ready for her and whoever's on the houseboat with her."

The video showed David turning the trolling motor off, and the boat continued to drift toward the houseboat with the wind. It showed him putting on rubber gloves, followed by a belt and gun holster. He holstered a Glock 9mm, pulled out a package of large cable ties and strapped them on his gun belt. He pulled a rag from his console and put in his left pants pocket, and then withdrew a dive knife with a leg strap sheath, which he secured to his right leg. He pulled the knife out with his right hand and held it close to the camera.

David said quietly, "This stainless dive knife is my favorite toy."

The video showed David turning the trolling motor back on and heading closer to the houseboat. A strong light shone on the upper deck of the houseboat to alert other boaters of the anchored houseboat. There was a low light on at the back of the lower deck, where a female could be seen laying on the chaise lounge. David turned the trolling engine off as he approached the houseboat, and picked up a line tied to the front cleat of his boat as he drifted quietly up to the houseboat. He grabbed the side rail and tied his boat's line to the rail. He scanned the top and bottom of the houseboat. The only noise was the loud air conditioning unit on the top of the houseboat that cooled the inside. David quietly boarded, and walked over to the female sleeping on the chaise lounge. As he got closer, he could see it was a shapely redhead sleeping on her back, spread eagle style, with her hands hanging off each side, and ankles spread towards each side. David said quietly, "Well, if it isn't her slutty friend from college, Susan."

David pulled out four cable ties and secured the red

head's wrists and ankles to the chaise lounge while she slept.

The video showed David opening the glass slider to the inside of the houseboat. The air conditioning vent on the ceiling became louder when he opened the door. There was a lamp turned on next to the couch where a tall blonde slept on her side in the fetal position. David stepped back to the open glass slider and said quietly, "It's her other college friend, the tramp, Lacy." David walked over and pulled out two cable ties. He carefully tied Lacy's ankles together and then her wrists. "Now, let's go find the bitch."

The video showed David walking through the inside of the houseboat, opening every closet and door. He then went upstairs and looked around the upper deck. He went back through the lower deck again, walked back outside, closed the sliders and looked at Susan tied up on the chaise lounge. David looked at Susan on her back in the yellow sun dress for about five seconds before he reached down and pulled his knife from his ankle sheath on his right calf. He put the knife up to her neck and moved it slowly to the left and cut the sundress strap, then he moved to the other side, and cut the second strap. He put the knife back in its sheath and stared at her sleeping for a few seconds. He grunted slightly and slowly pulled her dress down, exposing her breasts. He ran his fingers over both of Susan's nipples and then started caressing her breasts. After about 10 seconds of David squeezing Susan's breasts, she woke up, looking dazed and startled.

237

"What the hell! What are you doing here, David?" Susan blurted out as she tried to move, but couldn't because of the cable ties.

"Shut up, whore!" David said as he pulled the knife from his sheath, and put it in front of Susan's face, and slowly turned it.

Susan stopped struggling and glared at David and the knife. *"What have you done to Patricia?"*

David snickered and said menacingly, *"Don't play dumb with me—where's the bitch at?"*

"I don't know where she is," Susan said in a panicked tone. *"She brought us back from Cabbage Key earlier."*

There were a few seconds of silence before David said angrily, *"We can do this the easy way or the hard way, but you will tell me where Patricia is. So, I'm gonna ask you one more time—where's she at? You . . . will . . . tell me."*

Susan looked at the knife still in front of her face and pleaded, *"I don't know."*

"Ok, you get it the hard way."

The video showed David sheathing the knife. He pulled a rag from his left pants pocket and stuffed it in Susan's mouth, while she tried to scream. David pulled out his torch cigar lighter from his right pants pocket and flicked it on. He moved it toward Susan's nostrils and she tried to turn her head away, but he grabbed her forehead with his left hand, and held her head forward while he burned both nostrils

238

for a few seconds. Susan screamed, but the rag muffled her sounds. He closed the lighter and put it back in his right pants pocket before he pulled the rag out of her mouth, and put it on her belly.

"Where's she at?" David asked menacingly.

Susan pleaded. "I don't know—I swear!"

"More of the hard way!"

David picked up the rag from her belly and shoved it unceremoniously back in Susan's mouth, while she made muffled screams. David pulled out the lighter, flicked it on and moved it toward Susan's left nipple. Susan's eyes got very wide and she tried screaming harder, but the rag continued to muffle her sound. David burned her left nipple for about five seconds, and then moved to the right nipple for about five seconds. Susan's body was convulsing and she was arching her back in protest, but the cable ties kept her secure. Her face turned red and she started crying as he turned the lighter off and put it back in his right pants pocket. He pulled the rag out of Susan's mouth and she spat on his face.

Susan yelled, "You needle dick piece of shit! I hate you!"

David wiped the spit off his face, and he unsheathed the knife from his right calf as he growled angrily. He walked behind Susan and grabbed her red hair with his left hand, yanking her head back against the chaise lounge while

Susan sobbed. He held the knife close to her throat with his right hand.

David said forcefully, "This is your last chance, you miserable whore. Where's Patricia at?"

Susan spoke her final words in a defiant tone. "I hope she's fucking somebody that can finally satisfy her after all those years with you!"

The video showed David forcefully slicing Susan's neck, and blood squirted everywhere. David backed up a few feet, breathing heavy as he watched Susan's blood pump out of her sliced neck. David watched for a little over two minutes until she bled out, and her body slumped over in the chaise lounge. Still breathing heavily, he glanced all around the boat. After about 30 seconds, he opened the sliding door inside and looked at Lacy still passed out on the couch. The air conditioning was the only sound that could be heard on the video. After a few seconds, he closed the door and walked back over to Susan's body. He cut the sundress off of her body and put it in the pile of blood under the chair. He cut the cables from Susan's wrists and ankles, and threw the body overboard.

As he looked at the body floating in the water, David said, "That bitch must've had her boyfriend come and get her on his boat. I knew she was screwing that fishing guide from the marina. The private investigator I hired sent me a video of them talking, and I saw the way she smiled at him. I knew she was cheating on me."

David walked over and opened the sliding door to the inside, where Lacy was still passed out. He picked up the blood soaked sundress, walked into the cabin and squeezed blood over Lacy. After he threw the sundress overboard, he walked back in and cut the cable ties on Lacy's wrists and ankles and threw them overboard. He then took Lacy's limp right hand in his gloved hand, made her finger tips touch the knife handle, grabbed the blade with his gloved hands, and set it down beside Lacy. He then walked over to the sink and washed the blood off of his gloved hands and arms. He walked outside and shut the sliding door and untied the line to his boat. After he got in his boat, he pushed free, and started floating with the tide.

David said quietly, "I'm gonna call 911 and report the body floating in the water. When the cops come, they'll find blondie with the murder weapon and blood all over her. Let Patricia explain why her boat is still there when they find the body. Hopefully, they'll charge her as an accessory, and after she goes to prison, I won't have to pay any more alimony."

The video showed David switching on the trolling motor and quietly driving about a quarter mile away before he turned the trolling motor off. He then pulled the trolling motor up, secured it, and the boat drifted with the tide. He grabbed two large black plastic garbage bags. In the first

241

bag, he put the ankle sheath, rag, gun, gun belt, and holster. He then completely stripped down and put all of the bloody clothes, shoes, and his gloves in the second bag. He tied both bags and then put them in the front hatch. After he put the bags away, he took the GoPro camera off his head and put it on the front of the boat, and angled it to the rear of the boat, so it could continue to record his actions. He walked naked to the back of the boat and jumped overboard. He swam about 20 yards away from the boat and back to get any remaining blood off of him.

Unhitching a collapsible ladder from his dive platform at the rear of the boat, he pulled himself aboard, pulled the ladder up and secured it, walked to the front hatch, pulled out a towel and a gym bag. After he dried off, he opened the gym bag and changed into fresh clothes and shoes. He put the wet towel in the gym bag and put it back in the front hatch. He went to the front of the boat and put the GoPro camera back on his forehead. He then walked to the back of the boat and pulled out a bucket from the rear hatch. He used the bucket to scoop up salt water and throw it all over the boat to clean off any blood remnants on the boat. After he finished swabbing the deck, all of the water drained out the drainage holes, and he put the bucket away in the rear hatch. He opened up his cooler, grabbed a beer and twisted off the top. After a long drink, he opened his console, pulled out his cell phone from a dry bag, called 911, and reported a body floating.

After he finished the 911 call, he drained his beer and belched. The last thing on the video was him stating smugly, "No woman will ever get the better of me!"

Chapter 21

Friday, September 11, 2015 at 7:45 p.m.

Frank Power's condo in Ft. Myers, Florida

"What a day," Frank said wearily to Beth, sitting with him on his lanai, looking at the glowing sunset sparkling over the calm water. There were no clouds on the horizon, so the sun was making a mirror image reflection on the water.

Beth nodded and said quietly, "Tell me about it, honey. I want to hear what happened after we left your office."

Frank drained his scotch and set the empty glass on the table between them. Beth took a sip of her wine and looked at the sunset, which had reached the magical time when it was partially obstructed by the horizon and was sinking fast. Beth thought of her mom and her superstitious belief of being able to communicate with relatives at this time. Even though she doubted it was possible, she mentally sent her mom a message of love through the fading sunset.

Frank cleared his throat and took a deep breath. "The first thing I did was take Patricia's laptop with me to my

245

boss's office, told him the story, and we watched the video together. When we finished, he was silent for a few seconds before he said, 'Clean up this mess, ASAP. Call the defense lawyer and tell her everything. Then I want you to work on a press release with our public relations director. I want the charges dismissed and the press release given out today to all media outlets.' He shook his head and said ruefully, 'It makes me think back to other weak cases over the years that I handled, before video, and the wild stories some of the Defendants told on the stand. What if some of them were true and innocent people are rotting in prison?'"

Frank cleared his throat. "I assured my boss that even though we don't have a perfect criminal justice system, we have the best in the world. He agreed, but I could tell it was bothering him as he stared out his window in silence. So, I left his office and went back to my office, and called the Defendant's attorney, Amanda Blayne, and explained what had happened. I told her as soon as I hung up the phone with her, I was going to file a formal dismal of charges with the clerk's office and do a press release to all of the media outlets."

Beth snorted loudly and shook her head. "I bet that bitch was in heaven when she learned she won another case."

Frank sat up in his chair and said quietly, "Actually, she was very humble and asked if I could send her a copy of the video. I told her I would, but asked that she not release it to the media to protect the victim's relatives from more heartache. She readily agreed, and by the end of the conversation, she was sobbing and said she couldn't wait to tell Lacy. She said after they watched her copy of the video, she would destroy it."

Beth drained her wine glass and set it on the table next to Frank's empty glass. After a few seconds of reflection, Beth said philosophically, "I've always said that justice is a lot like sausage—everyone likes it, but no one wants to watch it being made."

Frank said in a jaded tone, "Very true."

After a few moments of them both looking silently at the sun disappearing on the horizon, Frank looked over at Beth and said earnestly, "We should get a dog together."

Chapter 22

The Veranda restaurant in Ft. Myers, Florida

Patricia walked into the Veranda and looked around to see if Lacy had arrived. When she didn't see her sitting in the bar area, she looked over at the hostess, who was on the phone taking reservations. Patricia was wearing a light blue madras dress from L.L. Bean with white sandals. She had died her hair back to her normal brunette color.

After the hostess hung up, she looked at Patricia and said cheerfully, "Can I help you?"

"Could I get a table for two in the bar area? I'm meeting a friend for drinks."

The hostess smiled. "Of course. Follow me."

The hostess seated Patricia at a table next to the ceiling-to-floor wine rack, about 10 feet from the piano bar, with a clear view to the front door. Patricia sat down, and a waitress walked up. "Can I get you a cocktail?"

Patricia thought for a second. "A martini with Grey Goose vodka and extra olives would be perfect."

"I'll be right back," the waitress said pleasantly.

Patricia relaxed in her chair, but she had butterflies in her stomach. Lacy and she had talked twice on the phone since the murder charge had been dismissed, but this was the first face-to-face meeting since then. The first phone call was the day after the charges had been dropped, and Lacy had been very tentative and guarded with Patricia. The second phone call a few days later was more pleasant, but Patricia could feel some hidden anger from Lacy. She felt terrible about the situation, and decided she and Lacy needed to have a meeting and discuss everything that had happened. Patricia wasn't sure how Lacy would act toward her, so she wanted the meeting in a public place. She suggested a happy hour at the Veranda and Lacy readily agreed.

The waitress brought the martini to the table and Patricia took a sip, feeling it tingle her throat as it went down. She was hoping some liquid courage would get her through this meeting with Lacy. Patricia had met Beth twice for lunch since the day they had gone to Frank's office and given him David's laptop. At their last lunch, Patricia had told Beth how remorseful she felt about staying in Belize while Lacy was on trial for her life. Beth suggested Patricia see a therapist to discuss her feelings and gave her the name of a therapist that had helped some of Beth's other clients. Patricia had taken Beth's advice and made an appointment to see the therapist the following week.

The front door to the Veranda opened, and Lacy walked in. Lacy was wearing a light purple sun dress with white pumps, and it looked like she'd been at the beach all day because she was freshly tanned and her blond hair was curly, like it had been blown in the wind. She looked around the bar and saw Patricia sitting at the table. Lacy gave her a small wave and a polite smile, and walked over to the table.

Patricia had a quick sip of her martini before she stood up as Lacy approached. Patricia smiled sincerely and said, "It's so good to see you."

Patricia leaned forward to give Lacy a hug, but Lacy stiffened. A moment later, Lacy slowly leaned in and gave a polite hug, but didn't squeeze Patricia's back with her hands. Patricia immediately sensed Lacy's reluctance, and quickly adjusted to reciprocate Lacy's reserved response. After their awkward embrace, they both sat down in embarrassed silence.

Fortunately, the waitress approached and broke the uncomfortable silence. "Can I get you a drink?"

Lacy said flatly, "A bottled water and a glass of ice."

As the waitress walked away, Patricia took a large drink of her martini. Lacy looked at Patricia's martini and said softly, "I haven't drunk since my arrest. I guess I'm a little gun shy about drinking since that night on the houseboat."

Patricia leaned forward and said sincerely, "I'm so sorry I put the ruffies in both of your drinks that night. I had no

251

idea that David would follow me out there."

Lacy was quiet for a moment and took a deep breath. "I realize that. However, since I watched the disgusting video he made, I sometimes wonder if I could've stopped it if I wasn't drunk. And drugged."

Patricia felt nauseous as she considered Lacy's answer. She had not focused on what would have happened that night if she hadn't left the houseboat, and they were all awake when David came to the houseboat. Her mind started racing with the possibilities.

Lacy crossed her hands on the table before she continued. "I debate with myself if we could've stopped David that night, if we'd been awake. I tried to convince myself we could've defended ourselves and killed him, but I know it's just wishful thinking. He had a gun and a knife, and we had nothing. He'd killed all of us and made an even more disgusting video."

The waitress brought the bottled water and glass of ice to the table. Both Patricia and Lacy were looking down and quiet, so the waitress just set them down and walked away quietly.

After a few uncomfortable seconds, Patricia said sadly, "I never should've brought both of you out on the houseboat. It's all my fault."

Lacy leaned forward and put her hand on Patricia's hand. "It's not your fault, Patricia. I know that, but it's very hard because all of my friends and patients look at me like I have leprosy. Even though the murder charge has been dropped, everyone heard all of my dirty laundry, and all of the stupid things I said and did over the years. They will never look at me the same way."

Patricia nodded. "I know what you mean. Whenever I walk down the street, I can see people pointing and whispering. I know they'll never look at me the same way, or treat me the same way."

Lacy picked up her bottled water and poured it in the glass of ice. After a long drink, she leaned back in her chair and said morosely, "I drove over to Miami yesterday and went to Susan's grave."

Patricia started to tear up. She wanted to say something, but nothing would come out of her mouth. She finally just looked down, put her head in her hands, and started to weep softly. Lacy stood up, walked around the table, and gave her a heartfelt hug. After a few seconds of pulling Patricia close, she leaned down and whispered in her ear, "I know it's hard. We all miss her."

Lacy released Patricia and sat back down in her chair. A few people on the other side of the bar looked at the women curiously.

After Patricia regained her composure, Lacy said quietly, "I have to know what you were thinking when you were hiding out in Belize and reading the news over the internet about the murder and the trial. What did you think happened on the houseboat? Did you think I killed Susan?"

Patricia pulled a Kleenex out of her purse and blew her nose. She looked at Lacy anxiously and said shamefully, "I didn't know what to think. I just know what I read over the internet, and the newspapers made you look very guilty. In my heart, I knew you didn't do it, but . . . Susan was dead, and you were the only person on the boat when I left. I was very confused, and I had a lot of conflicting emotions. Part of me wanted to come back and ask you what happened, but another part of me was still scared of David, and I liked being away from him. I know it was selfish, but I was terrified of David and I had to stay away. It felt so good to finally be away from him, and I didn't want to lose that."

Lacy took a deep breath before she responded in a solemn tone. "The first time I watched the video, I was so stunned I could barely focus on the details. And then, I watched it three more times. Each time, I saw more details, and realized how much Susan suffered and how lucky I was to still be alive. But then to wake up, see your friend's neck sliced open . . . and face a murder charge for doing it. And not knowing what happened because I was drugged."

Lacy shook her head and Patricia felt her face flush with embarrassment. Patricia picked up her martini and drained it, hoping for some relief, but it just burned her belly as it mixed with the bile in her stomach.

254

Lacy leaned forward and said sincerely, "I forgive you. I know you never meant for any of this to happen.

Patricia looked up hopefully and said softly, "Really?"

Lacy nodded and said earnestly, "Yes, I forgive you."

About the Author

John D. Mills is a fifth generation native of Ft. Myers, Florida. He grew up fishing the waters of Pine Island Sound and it's still his favorite hobby. He graduated from Mercer University in Macon, Georgia with a BBA in Finance and worked for Lee County Bank in Ft. Myers for five months. He returned to Macon and graduated from Mercer's law school in 1989.

He started his legal career as a prosecutor for the State Attorney's Office in Ft. Myers. In 1990, he began his private practice concentrating in divorce and criminal defense.